The Monkey's Other Paw

REVIVED CLASSIC STORIES OF DREAD AND THE DEAD

EDITED BY
LUIS ORTIZ

nonstop press • new york

THE MONKEY'S OTHER PAW

Edited by Luis Ortiz

For Luisa

First Edition

Interior Illustrations & Book design by Luis Ortiz
Production by Nonstop Ink

Trade Paper: ISBN 978-1933065-33-5
Hardcover: ISBN 978-1-933065-62-5

PRINTED IN THE UNITED STATES OF AMERICA

www.nonstoppress.com

Contents

The Monkey's Other Paw

REVIVED CLASSIC STORIES OF **DREAD** AND THE **DEAD**

Introduction
These Will Chill You

_____

Luis Ortiz

Once upon a time — while still a child — I read a paperback book that seemed to me as terrifying as anything a nervous boy could imagine in a dark bedroom in the middle of the night. The book, which I then saw as a scary simulacrum of the mysterious world beyond my bedroom, was wrapped in a cover that appeared to be finger-painted in fresh blood. *These Will Chill You*, edited by Richard G. Sheehan and Lee Wright, and published in 1967 by Bantam Books, was a creepy amalgam of horror stories whose central concept was a visceral storytelling from the *Weird Tales* school of fiction. The book, inviting nightmares to a young, still forming mind, was a collage of sinister houseflies, ravenous rats, doomed characters, mysterious neighbors, torture devices, and other dreadful oddments. As a boy I read a good deal of horror and science fiction. As an adult, I have become a little more leery of grotesqueries, and have grown to be more captivated by non-fiction. But I still do get an intoxicating pleasure in re-reading the old stuff, and new fiction that riffs on some of the classic horror tropes.

An aging reader cannot but notice how fictional themes he remembers, with changing chronological perspectives, still serve as templates to generate new stories. (This is more apparent in television and movies.) Primal fears may disappear, to some degree, as we mature and our lives settle into some strata of civilized reality, but some of us still wake up in a cold sweat from the same nightmares we have had since childhood. Like a nightmare many of the stories from Sheehan and Wright's book still remain in my mind as clearly as the first time I read them.

My design for the *The Monkey's Other Paw* was: have modern authors of fantastika create new sequels, prequels, *hommages*, and re-imaginings to memorable classic supernatural horror stories. Among the stories selected were: "The Monkey's Paw," H.P. Lovecraft's "The Call of Cthulhu," Dylan Thomas' ghost story "The Followers," E.T.A. Hoffmann's "The Sandman," Robert Louis Stevenson's "Strange Case of Dr Jekyll and Mr Hyde," Octavio Paz' "The Blue Bouquet." Saki's "The Open Window," and — of course a book like this must also include the master — in this case Poe's unfinished story "The Lighthouse."

"The supernatural which persisted always in legends hand-ed down from one generation to another on the lips of living people had not lost its power to thrill and alarm, and gradu-ally worked its way back into literature." This is from Edith Birkhead's introduction to *The Tale of Terror* (1921). Poe ap-pears to be the first writer to distill all of the vital elements necessary for the modern horror tale from the muddle of his tormented psyche and bits and pieces of narratives that came to his erudite attention. As a commercial writer Poe was also smart enough to know that he needed to write stories that garnered attention — and horror and the supernatural did the trick for the audience of his day; the same audience that would flock to see the Cardiff Giant in upstate New York, or the Fegee Mermaid at P.T. Barnum's American Museum (or Barnum's House of Humbug, as critics named it), or show up as spectators at ghoulish public executions. Poe was influenced by the weird and spiritual nature of Nathaniel Hawthorne's fiction, just as Poe affected Lovecraft. This is the essence of horror stories, their hand-me-down nature.

Time does weird things to our memory and the stories from *These Will Chill You* may not all hold up to resurrection. I have reread only a few of those stories since childhood — the Sturgeon, Woolrich and Brennan — but I will go as far as saying that Sheehan and Wright's long out-of-print book is worth the search in the usual online and physical second-hand book stalls. And, of course, *These Will Chill You* was the seminal inspiration for the collection you now hold in your hands. There is no direct relationship to any of the stories from that book here — instead I have tried to capture some of the cosmic unease and stark fear that I felt in the very first collection of tales of terror that I ever read. I hope the readers of this book are all young enough in spirit to enjoy this new collection.

Here is the table of contents from *These Will Chill You*:

The Unheimlich Maneuver

Damien Broderick

Cocaine really was the bees' knees, safe yet soaringly efficacious. It sent Freud's mind whirring, powered him through sleepless nights of research and uneasy insight. Finally, though, he now felt ready to crash. He dismissed his nurse and his receptionist, lay back on the brocaded couch reserved for his patients and, as anticipated, dreams, nightmares and vapors of eternity rushed about his closed eyes.

In the instantaneous transition of dream, the alienist gazed down from a tall building exactly like this 13 story steel, brick, glass, and oak medical center recently built at Berggasse 19, in the ninth district, by Tesla Gesellschaft. From his 11th floor consulting room, and through his bearded, fragmented, floating reflection in the leaded casement's glass, Freud saw something that sent a thrill through his flesh. It moved far below in the busy street. He took up the new electrical field glasses presented to him by his most famous patient, pressed them to his eyes. In and out of the scurrying pedestrians, gentlemen in frock coats and toppers, haughty fashionable ladies in immense bustles like ships under sail, servants in dirndl-gewand, buggies, Fiacres, charabancs, cabriolets, officers on horseback, and a few honking Teslaforce-powered horseless carriages spitting sparks, a curious gray bush actually seemed as if it were *striding toward him.* Freud shuddered, and redoubled his pacing in the woods under the spinning shape of the zeppelin.

Piercingly sharp tones brought him bolt upright from the couch. Zeppelin? What? But no, it was the Teslaphon, piping him from sleep, as hectoring and demanding as a patient in deep transference. He snatched up the headset, clapped its cool Lamenite over his ears.

"It's Fließ. You free to talk?"

"Dude!"

"I'll take that for a ja. Hey, that invert thing at the conference about da Vinci? You totally fucked up."

Straight into it, no small talk with Wilhelm Fließ. Unless

he was soothing you into a therapeutic hypnotic trance, or poking around in your nose, and that was hardly chit-chat anyway.

"What would you know about da Vinci, you dabbler? I've been studying the man's work for years." Freud was genuinely nettled, he realized.

"Leonardo's dream. It wasn't a vulture."

"Of course it was. The significance of the Egyptian mother goddess Mut is obvious, dummkopf. *Der Geier*, a vulture. With its tail feathers opening the kid's mouth. How homoerotic do you want a dream to be?"

"*Nibbo*, not *geier*," Fließ said. "A kite. Wrong myth, *meshuggah*."

Immediately, like a thunderbolt, Freud understood the magnitude of his goof. And it struck him that he and his whimsical younger friend were speaking in the louche Viennese German of his childhood, picked up in school after the family relocated from Freiberg in Moravia. Crushed, he crossed to the window and stared down into the street. Traffic was incessant. The shadow of a zeppelin passed slowly across the nearby red-tiled roofs. The world was changing fast.

Fließ said, "How's the monograph doing? Man, coke's gotta be more gripping than carving up 900 eels looking for their balls."

"Trust me. Yeah, the cocaine treatise's getting a respectful hearing. At least there won't be any scandal with this topic."

"But listen, bro," Fließ said, "how's your pal Brueur's Miss Pappenheim? Still got it together after the breakup?"

"Totally."

"Awesome."

"But man, let's not call Bertha by her real name, not even in private. Anna O."

"Whatever."

The heavy headset was squeezing his ears, as if someone invisible stood behind him, pressing hard; he shifted it, and his ears throbbed, his eyes watered, his nose tingled. Nasal reflex neurosis. Time for more cocaine treatment. "I'm guessing there's some reason you called."

"I have a patient you might consider taking on. Very interesting case. Talk about hysteria. Can I send this cat over?"

Freud leafed through his appointment book. "I have an opening Tuesday week at... hmm... after lunch. Two o'clock?"

"Dynamite."

Day was fading. Freud activated the gas lamps, and in the brightening light reached for his casebook, drawing his pen and ink toward it. If he failed to jot down at least the fundamentals of his oracular dream, it would be lost.

"Come in, young man," Freud said. He did not extend his hand. "I expected an introductory referral from your otorhinolaryngologist, Dr. Fließ, but the mail's been delayed for the last several days. Now, you are—" He took up his pen, leaned to the casebook open on his desk.

"Frantz Travesti," the patient mumbled in a French accent, then covered his mouth with his free hand. The other held a book. "A joke. I am Nathaniel Bernhardt."

Freud shifted effortlessly to formal French. "No relation

to the celebrated Sarah?"

"You might say I'm her son."

"I see." Freud jotted a note, keeping his features expressionless. Bernhardt, or more likely "Bernhardt," was a striking if somewhat androgynous fellow, hardly beyond 20 or 21, and his strong nose did indeed rather resemble that of the great actress—who, though surely by coincidence, had been wildly infatuated with Nikola Tesla. (Or was that what had brought the boy here, via Fließ as an attempted feint?) Of course Tesla had repudiated her yearnings. Freud had satisfactorily cured the inventor's molysomophobia, his neurotic terror of physical contact and attendant infection, but Nikola remained obdurately resistant to sexual expression.

"Not literally," Nathaniel said. "You might say I am her spiritual child. I am an actor and dancer."

"A travesti, then," Freud murmured. "Adopting the role of a female on stage, as your namesake not infrequently takes the role of a man, Hamlet, for example."

Astonished, the young fellow gazed at the alienist. "Absolutely correct, sir. But this season I am not in women's costume. I have the role of, of…" He faltered.

"Frantz, in Delibes' *Coppélia,* yes."

The young man relaxed a little. "Ah. I see you have had a report from Dr. Fließ after all. Or have you been to the theater and seen me on stage with your own eyes?"

"Neither. A series of inferences or scientific inductions, Mr. Bernhardt. You carry a volume of Hoffmann's *Phantasiestücke in Callots Manier.* Granted your profession—"

"Ah," said Nathaniel, "ah. You are astute. May I take my place upon your famous couch? I feel somewhat… faint."

"By all means," Freud said. "You may hang your coat on the stand over there. The shoes, please remove them. You may cover your feet with the rug if you feel cold. A joke is no joking matter, jests and dreams are the royal roads to the unconscious. Frantz is the luckless protagonist in the operetta. You see yourself foreshadowed *avant la lettre* in Hoffmann's story?"

Nathaniel shuddered theatrically. "More than you could possibly imagine, doctor." He put the book on the floor at his side, lay down with a certain epicene grace. "I have begun to remember the most horrific events from my childhood. And now, now that I, that I—"

Freud took the chair behind the patient's head. Commentators in the press sometimes speculated that this position was chosen to allow his patients the free expression of their every thought, without the authoritative and censorious gaze of the analyst burning into their own undefended eyes. It was not so, of course. Freud permitted himself an undetected smile. No, it was simply that he could not tolerate being stared at by other people for eight hours or more a day. On the whole, he had found little that was "'good'" about human beings. In his experience most of them were trash, no matter whether they publicly subscribed to this or that ethical doctrine, or to none at all. They enacted the urgings of their instincts, base and wholesome alike, no better than wind-up mechanisms set free to roam the streets. But that was something you could not say aloud, or perhaps even think.

Freud had allowed the moment of strangled silence to extend long enough. "There is something you cannot say aloud? The very purpose of our sessions, sir, is to give you absolute *carte blanche* to utter whatever comes to your lips, however it might seem to stray from the purpose, however disgraceful, depraved or simply boring it strikes you. I myself shall say very little, Mr. Bernhardt—"

The patient twisted, looking over his shoulder. "Please call me Nathaniel."

"Very well, Nathaniel. Now lie back and gaze at the ceiling. Allow your thoughts to wander where they will, and your tongue to give them free expression."

Another silence. "Really, I don't know where to begin."

"Recall some vivid and meaningful event. You just told me that you have been troubled by memories of the most horrific events from your childhood."

"Yes. Yes. And more recently. Oh, dear God—"

"First, childhood. Close your eyes, if you wish. You are perfectly safe and protected here, Nathaniel."

"Where's your pad? Aren't you meant to be taking notes?"

Freud said, "I do not take notes. It is distracting. I need to keep my attention focused on what you will say. Now let us begin."

"My father was a professor of… anatomy at the University of Paris," the young man said. "His name was Alessandro…" Again he hesitated. "Well, Bernhardt, obviously. My mother is Maria Josephina, and I have no sisters, and just one brother, Sigismund."

Freud's lips tightened involuntarily. But the youth was not

addressing him, not with such easy familiarity. So Sigismund was Nathaniel's brother's name. But there had been resistance. Alessandro was no name for a Frenchman. Something was being hidden. It was sheer coincidence that Freud's own given name had been Sigismund, until he changed it to Sigmund when he was 22, working hard on his doctorate at the University of Wein. It was not a common name, certainly not among the French, for all its heraldic virtue—"protection through victory"; Freud felt the faintest uncanny shiver.

"We seldom saw father," the young man was saying. "He ate separately from us boys, came home late from his laboratory, went straight upstairs without a word to us, either to his study or the marital bed. In the morning, when we prepared for school, he was either gone or kept his own counsel. But we heard his passage on the stairs, as we tussled after dinner or finished our homework beneath mother's stern eye, his steady tread and the squeaking of the steps. And then later, as we made ready for bed, the further squeaking and crashing of another pair of boots..." He broke off, said nothing for a time.

"Mother sent us up to bed with the injunction, 'Off you go now, the Sandman will visit you soon. He'll sprinkle sand in your sleepy eyes and send you off to dream land.' Sigismund and I puzzled over this, half excited, half shuddering, until it occurred to me that this heavy tread up to father's study was the Sandman. I asked our nurse one day who this Sandman is, and she gave me a look of horror, or pretended horror. 'Oh, little boy, he is a very wicked fellow, who visits bad children when they refuse to go to bed, and throws sharp grinding sand into their face, until their eyes burst bleeding from their heads. He hides these eyes in his bag and flies them up to the crescent moon to feed his children.' 'Oh no!' I cried, filled with horror and terror, and little Sigismund burst into frightened tears. I put my arms around him, crying myself. 'Oh yes,' said Nanny, 'those children of the Sandman perch by moonlight in their nest in the sky, and with their crooked beaks they pick up the eyes of the bad human children, and gobble them for their supper.'"

With frantic abruptness, Nathaniel sat up straight on the couch, flung his feet to the floor, and turned a piteous, bleached face to the alienist. "That was the man who visited my father in the night, and worked with him in his laboratory. The Sandman. The Sandman."

Freud glanced at his clock. It seemed longer, but they had been at it less than half an hour.

"Pray settle yourself, sir," he said. "We rehearse memories and fancies and phantasies in analysis, yet these have no power to harm us. As children, yes, such images might bring our eyes almost literally starting from our heads. But now we are men, and know that dreams or nightmares can bring us to treasures of self-knowledge but they cannot hurt us. Please lie down again, young man, and resume your recollections. Or feel free to change the subject. The only requirement here is that you will utter your associations freely, without hindering them, without embroidery. And now, let us resume."

Two or three minutes of obstinate mutescence followed, and Freud heard only the stertorous breathing of a man in deep pain. He bit his lip and said nothing. Finally Nathaniel spoke again, and now his voice held the false calm and clarity of a theatrical on a stage ringed with gas lights.

"I have said nothing yet, doctor, of my true horror. One evening, goaded by curiosity, I crept upstairs from my bedroom and hid inside a closet in father's study. Laboratory, rather. It was a large, long room, filled with glass vessels and pieces of dead creatures floating inside jars and acids and other dangerous substances, and at the far end a hooded enclosure fitted with a dull iron box as large as a coffin, serviced by pipes for gas. Despite my anticipation, I drifted off to sleep, and woke only at the double tread of feet, like the stamping of twins in a march, rising up the stairs. The door creaked open, and slammed closed. Night was falling; a single gas mantle gave sepulchral lighting to the room. I saw my father put on a heavy protective garment of rubber, and help his companion into one similar. They bent over the coffin, sighing, muttering, and fired up a blaze of purple light that flickered and settled into a steady, uncanny glow. I could not quite see the Sandman's face, but his shoulders were broad and his hands, when they fell into the light, dark with thick hair. "Coppelius," my father said, "we are all but complete in our work, but we have no eyes." They stood back and I seemed to see lifeless human faces without eyes, just deep dark holes penetrating the flesh above their cheeks. "We need human eyes, living eyes!" this Coppelius groaned. I screamed, and dashed from my hiding place. The Sandman took hold of me and dragged me to the coffin, which now seemed filled with flame. "Here are eyes," he cried to my father, "a handy pair of child's eyes." He drew with his tongs from the flame some red-hot grains, intent on flinging them into my eyes. My father shouted his horrified objection, "No, you must leave my son Nathaniel his eyes!" Coppelius laughed, and said: "Yes, very well, I'll leave his eyes, he'll need them to weep, but let us at least examine the machinery of his hands and feet." He seized me so forcibly that my joints cracked, and screwed off my hands and feet, and then put them on again, one here and the other there. The room went altogether dark, a cramp took me, and I lost all feeling. I was not quite lost to consciousness, though. I heard my father cry in rage—or was it Coppelius?—and an explosion shook the laboratory, then another, and fire rained down upon us all, took hold of the heavy curtains and walls. When I woke I was lying, cold and dripping in the street, my mother insensible with grief, the house almost entirely devoured by flames. They told me that Sigismund was safe, but that my father had perished in the flames. Of the Sandman there was no smallest sign. No one had set eyes on him as he arrived, or if he left. The magistrates concluded later that no visitor had been there, that my father's reckless experiments brought about his fate, and ours, and that if any other *had* visited us that night, he was either long gone or had perished in the same fire that burned the flesh from my father's hands and face and boiled away his poor eyes."

High, luminously clear air parted with the mildest purr before the teardrop prow of the *Friedrichshafen* out of Berlin, now cruising above the blue, blue waters of the Danube. Green and brown fields stretched to the horizon on every side. Now and then they passed over a quaint village, and invariably the yokels and children ran about to gaze upward, agog, waving their hats and crying wordlessly. He could never have afforded such luxury, such *frivolity*, had not he and Breuer been sent an engraved and signed invitation from the desk of Tesla himself. Was he anxious at this elevation above his adopted country, this taunting of fate in the fashion of Icarus? A little, Freud confessed to himself, but only a little. Yes, zeppelins had crashed, crumpled, burst terribly into flame—but that was in the early days, years ago now, when Count Zeppelin's craft had employed hydrogen for lift, rather than the safe, inert helium urged by Tesla. The reflection made his lips quirk. Hydrogen, the element of water, burned like the flames of Hell, while the essence of sunlight, helium, isolated in air only after its absorption line had been plucked out of a spectrograph of the Sun, was entirely placid, coolly so.

"*Schnapps*, my friend?" asked Breuer, gesturing to the smartly uniformed flight attendant. Freud nodded, still abstracted, and the fellow crossed the rich carpet and poured them each a glass. The craft flowed through the sky without bump or rattle, unlike the thundering locomotives that now crisscrossed Europe. The powerful engines at the rear of its great gasbag thrummed, but the vibration seemed somehow comforting, like a mother's calm breath in the ear of a babe nursing at her breast. Freud threw back his drink and regarded his older comrade. Of late, he sensed a certain falling out between them. The poor man still suffered from his infatuation with Miss Pappenheim—with "Anna O." he corrected himself—and the strain on his marriage seemed to have clouded his faith in their developing techniques for healing the neurotic spirit.

"A capital adventure," Freud said, setting down his glass. With Breuer, he adopted Hochdeutsch solemnity, none of the jocose slang that gave his conversations with Fließ their merry piquancy. He glanced at the aristocrats and high military officers and their ladies reclining in comfort, set elegantly against the mahogany and brass fittings, feet resting confidently on the thick carpet. "If only our brides could have shared it."

"I grant you, Mathilde sent me a foul look as I departed. Still, I'm confident that the ladies and our little chickens will enjoy a fine day together."

Freud reached for a cigar, bit his lip in frustration. Prohibited, even with the benefit of helium; no risk of fire at altitude might be countenanced.

"In any event, Josef," he said, "I mean this to be more than a pleasure trip. I have a strange story to discuss with you. I would welcome your advice." Breuer leaned forward, hearing this, his high forehead gleaming in the sunlight from their large glazed porthole. "It concerns a most disturbed young man who was sent to me several weeks ago by Fließ."

Quickly, in lowered tones he felt sure could not be overheard by the other parties, he sketched the unpleasant fairytale with which Nathaniel's nurse had wounded his sleep and indeed his childhood. Hearing of the fire that had consumed the father, Breuer grimaced. "Still and all," the older man said, "we have all heard such horrid tales in our vulnerable infancy. I myself recall the horripilation with which my flesh greeted the tale of the sisters who cut off their own toes and heels—"

"Yes, indeed," Freud said, "but the story becomes far more peculiar and convoluted. Are you familiar with the macabre tales of E.T.A. Hoffmann?"

"Only via the ballet of Delibes. Something about a doll, a

clockwork creation that comes to life? A young girl who masquerades as the doll?"

"My patient is a theatrical," Freud said. "He has performed in this work. And now he believes himself infatuated with such a doll. But let me draw out the tale as it was delivered to me."

Nathaniel, he explained, was an apparently healthy if rather dreamy young fellow barely done with his schooling, not noticeably scarred by his traumatic memory or phantasy, engaged to a charming young woman from his own town, one Clara. No great beauty, Clara was, even so, much admired by the locals, petitioned by all the swains, ready to smile or laugh, gay with dancing, a fine cook, ready for a husband. She had set her eyes on Nathaniel (assuming his account to be true), and he responded to her interest, finally asking her father for her hand. But a curious stranger had come to the township and set up business as a mechanic, an optician and telescope maker, bringing with him his own extraordinarily beautiful daughter. This shy creature, Olympia, was rarely permitted to leave the house. The first time he saw her, Nathaniel was struck dumb with admiration. Passion flamed in his breast. Only one thing held him from breaking his engagement with Clara and declaring himself to Olympia's father—an equal and opposite horror stirred in him by the very sight of the man.

This worthy, he was convinced, was none other than the fiendish Coppelius who had tried to steal his eyes, and whose machinations had brought about his father's death.

"Uncanny!" said Breuer with a slight shiver.

"Exactly!" cried Freud, then lowered his voice again, abashed by the glances of his fellow travelers. "But precisely, the very word. *Unheimlich*! The very contrary of our sweet, comforting, homely *Heimlich*! A conjuncture to put a chill at the edge of one's neck, a shudder in our limbs."

Breuer smiled, perhaps embarrassed by his own reaction. "Well, Sigmund, perhaps not quite so dramatic as that."

"Oh yes, much more so. Wait for the rest of the tale!"

Nathaniel was obsessed. He moved to a room situated across from the optician's residence, cunningly finding a window that looked directly into Olympia's own quarters. Steeling himself, he purchased a fine pair of opera glasses from the man whose very visage filled him with terror and a determination to have his revenge. Yet he could not kill Olympia's father without forfeiting her love. Each night he sat for hours at his window, hidden by drapes, and watched the beautiful girl who sat in her night attire, almost motionless, gazing out from her own window as if directly at him. Her eyes had a dreamy abstraction that appealed to his poetic soul, but he also found them… uncanny, yes, the very word he used in telling his tale from the couch—*Unheimlich*! For she rarely blinked. There seemed a kind of deadness in her regard that he yearned to kindle into life, to bring back to her stifled soul that very liveliness which had once enchanted him in Clara.

Finally he met her at a grand party her father held to introduce himself and his daughter to the town, and to extend his business contacts. The fellow had the instincts of a merchant, vulgar in the extreme, mounting outside his dwelling a large painted advertisement portraying an immense pair of Teutonic blue eyes behind glass, a blade of light caught above each lens, and an admonition:

EYES! PRETTY EYES!

The very sight of that uncouth billboard brought acid to the throat of the youth, but his devotion, his obsession with the girl Olympia made him choke it back, dress in his best, cross the street when the gas lights were lit, and mingle with the crowds who arrived on foot and by carriage, passing by his host at the entrance with only the most fleeting touch of his gloved hand. Coppelius, if it were truly he, nodded and smiled with his ugly yellow teeth, and Nathaniel moved in a daze into the fire-hot sweaty confusion and babble of the gathering.

Olympia sat motionless, in pale blue and white. He approached her with trepidation but conviction, bowed, took her hand—her icy cold hand—and raised her fingers to his lips. She met his gaze with a dispassion that thrilled him. When the waltz began, she rose at his invitation and moved into his arms, treading the measures with perfect regularity, murmuring to his whispered declarations "Ah! Ah!" and nothing more.

Finally, shaking with emotion, he allowed her to move into the proffered arms of another young swain, and watched somewhat bitterly from the side as first one and then another competed for her attention. With growing rage he watched their expressions change, from restrained lust to surprise and then to mockery, saw them huddle together after they relinquished her, laughing with ribald derision, casting glances across at him, gesturing obscenely with their thrusting fingers. He wished he had a saber to lay about, cutting their nasty fingers from their hands, jabbing their scornful eyes—

Later, as the music ebbed, Nathaniel reclaimed her, held her coolness against his breast, rubbed warmth into her hands. Her face was angelic, impassive as a mask, almost holy. Finally the gas lamps yielded to dimness, candles guttered, the hall was empty. He handed daughter to father, with a curt, confused bow, and escaped into the chilly, moonlit night.

From his window, holding the glass to his burning eyes, he watched Olympia settle into her seat, upright, motionless. Her father entered the room, and stripped her icy blue and white garments from her pale limbs. Leaves moved in a wind to obscure the wickedness Nathaniel thought he witnessed, but in a moment of sheer horror—the true *unheimlichkeit* that can bring up a man's hairs stiff upon his neck and arms— he saw Coppelius reach toward her waxen face and tear out her eyes. The optician turned, then, and sent a look of triumph toward his window, as if he saw the youth behind his curtains, or perhaps the gleam of the edge of the moon cast back by the lenses of his opera glass. The father turned away, leaving her there in her chair, all but unclad, face empty, black eye sockets emptier still.

In the warm golden afternoon, the airship moved across the outskirts of Wein. Freud peered down through the great window extending across at the back of the cabin, where he and Breuer had repaired with their wine. Mile after mile of ancient buildings, elegant and sumptuous mid-19th century apartments, the late century skyscrapers, as they were hubristically dubbed, pioneered by Tesla Gesellschaft. He sipped, resting his voice.

"Always the eyes," Breurer said quietly. "And what is your interpretation of this mutilation, Sigmund? We all dread the loss of our senses, but I suspect that you find something sexual at the root of your patient's obsessions."

"Indeed. I have been reading Sophocles again, Josef."

"Ah. *Oedipus Rex.*"

"Why is it that Oedipus tears out his eyes? And Shakespeare's King Lear? Their transgressions are sexual, certainly, and, more than that, they are familial. They must pay with their eyes for the damage they have done to their lineage. And really, Josef, in phantasy what are eyes, if not—"

"Balls," Breuer said coarsely.

"Precisely. It is symbolic castration—in this case, auto-castration, but it defers and yet seeks to acknowledge the dread a son holds toward the father, the judgmental gaze of the father, the lustful sight the father possesses of the mother, whom the child desires above all else, the fear of the truncating knife. It is phallic to the very root." He reached into his pockets. "Dear God, I hope we land soon."

"A cigar, Sigmund?" Breuer sent him a sidelong, vaudeville look.

"Sometimes a cigar is only—" Freud began with some asperity, paused, went on, "is the only thing that gets us through the day. Anyway, I'm changing my procedure for once. I've invited the boy to bring this young paragon of beauty and genital menace to meet me on Tuesday at our next consultation."

"He'll turn up alone, and pretend to have forgotten the arrangement."

"Presumably. But what a bayonet-cut this will make in his defenses!"

The *Friedrichshafen* lowered slowly from the heavens, Icarus redeemed. The tear of an angel as large as the sky, a ship fallen from another planet. Or something Faust might have yearned after, abandoning his soul. Freud moved toward the debarkation door, rubbing his tired, smarting eyes.

"Mr. Bernhardt is here to see you, doctor," his receptionist said. She was fifty, and plain. "And he has a… an associate with him. Shall I show them both in?"

"Please do, Hannah." Freud rose from his desk, greeted his patient, then bowed over the glorious young woman's outstretched hand. It was cool, but not freezing cold. For an instant he caught that reflection as it passed through the outskirts of his mind, and thought, I am becoming caught up in his delusions. "Sit here," he said, showing them to a pair of simple chairs, turning his own at his desk to face them. And you are Miss…?"

"Olympia Spallanzani," she said in German with the faintest trace of Italian. Her nose was strong in her lovely face. With shock, Freud looked again from one to the other. They might have been doubles, allowances made for sex and dress. A cousin? A *sister*? Nathaniel had denied having a sister. Why deny it if it were true?

"Thank you for coming in with Mr...." He let his voice fade for a moment. "...Bernhardt," he said.

"Come, sir, you know now that I prevaricated. I am Nathaniel Spallanzani, son of the artificer Alessandro Spallanzani, great nephew of the physiologist Lazzaro Spallanzani."

Freud turned, jotted a note. "I know that name. He was a priest and a celebrated biologist, as you say." He frowned. "But that was more than a century ago. He disproved the spontaneous generation of life."

The young woman uttered a jejune laugh.

"I'm surprised that a man of the mind would know the work of a biologist," Nathaniel Spallanzani said. "Are you also aware that he studied spontaneous regeneration in the newt, and fertilized frog eggs on glass—*in vitro*?"

"You might not be aware, either," Freud said with some sharpness, "that my initial training was in neurology. The mind and its instincts are governed by the ancient history of the body. Yes, I am aware of your ancestor's important work, although it has fallen out of favor in this century. And you, miss," he added without any change of inflection, "you must be Mr. Spallanzani's sister."

The doll-like face creased in a foolish smirk.

"*La madre degli stronzi è sempre incinta!*" snarled the youth, and sprang forward, drawing from his coat pocket a length of thin, tough twine. He clouted the alienist across the head with a clenched fist, stunning him, and trussed him into his chair like a turkey ready for the oven. Freud swam in confusion. He reached for translation. The mother of assholes, he thought, is always pregnant.

"You think I fuck my sister? You simpleton. Here, look, look!"

The young man dragged the girl to her feet, seized her long garment, flung it up and over her face. Her naked body was revealed, without underclothing of any kind. Between her legs, Freud saw in numb confusion, was nothing but a smooth waxen ovoid, like a store dummy. As he passed into unconsciousness, Nathaniel ranted on, his chatter fading into clumps of meaningless sound.

As evening drew the last light from the sky, lamps came on in the street far below. Nathaniel had fallen silent, finally, and Freud felt himself, incredibly, slipping back into a doze. The soft huff as his twin gas lamps came on, at either end of his consulting room, drew him back to painful alertness. He tried to fix his attention on anything other than the pain of his arms, pulled tight behind his chair, and his feet, strapped to the foot of the couch. The lovely soft glow of the lamps reminded him of moonlight through mist, and that caused a momentary shudder. The Sandman and his vile children, perched on the hook of the crescent Moon... He turned his head deliberately and gazed at the nearest lamp. An Austrian, he thought with justifiable civic pride, had invented that clever hood, that mantle, diffusing and retaining the burning gas. Carl Auer von Welsbach. How astute his mind was, to recall that name in these dire circumstances. Freud smiled at his own puff of pride. He had met Welsbach less than two years ago, dining with Tesla and his glamorous entourage. Charming as ever, Tesla had nonetheless managed to mention with his own expression of pride the electrical lighting he was developing with the American, Edison. Why, if —

A tapping at the door. "Doctor," he heard faintly, through the sturdy oak timbers, "I must go home now. I shall come back tomorrow and complete the cleaning."

The madman was at his side, glowering. "Not a word," he said quietly. "Not one word."

Freud met his eyes. "Thank you, and good evening to you, Mrs. Holzknecht," he called in a raised voice. "You can finish your work tomorrow morning."

"Good night, doctor."

"Mr. Spallanzani," Freud said then, "you must release me immediately. You are upset, I understand that perfectly."

"Not perfectly," the madman said. His eyes were blackly shining in the gas light.

"I need press no charges if we leave here directly. No purpose is being served—"

Spallanzani, if that was truly his name, laughed. "So you imagine. But I have not yet completed my story. You think me disturbed, doctor? It is you who will be disturbed when you learn the full degree of my relationship with the lovely Olympia."

Freud moved his head. The girl was slumped in her chair, breast rising and falling in a mechanical rhythm. Was it truly possible that the creature was not a maimed human but a lifeless mechanism, like the doll in Hoffmann's uncanny tale? His thought reeled. The writer had penned his phantasies in the first decades of the century. He was much traveled—had he met Lazzaro Spallanzani? Surely not, the old biologist must have died around the time Hoffmann was born. But Lazzaro's brother—was he a twin?—had fathered children, and one of those, in turn, had lived to father the poor madman who held him captive. Were his hallucinations and nightmares in some sense true? Why, how could he even doubt it? The impeccable but *Unheimlich* automaton crooning in its chair was proof entire.

In the silence of the empty building, there came abruptly a thunderous banging on the door.

The constabulary, Freud thought with a rush of relief, and felt himself sagging against his tight restraints. Martha has realized—

But the madman had turned, eyes shining with delight. He rushed to the door, found the key, turned it, flung the door open. From the corner of his eye, Freud could see only darkness in the hallway. He strained his neck, turned as far as he might. No policeman spoke in gruff, authoritative tones. Two dark shapes stood at the boundary, neither moving. One was a man, shorter it seemed than Nathaniel Bernhardt. The madman was all but capering with excitement, inviting his visitors in with extravagant gestures. The other was a, a, gray bush that *moved*, impelled, he saw with disbelief, by its own locomotion, as if it were an animal or worse, moved forward from the darkness slowly into the room.

The alienist shrank against the back of his chair, a scream rising inside his breast but choked off.

Dear God, he thought in confusion, it is Don Giovanni's baleful, animated statue of the Commendatore, come to drag me down to hell.

As it drew closer to him the thing changed its shape, extended branches into arms, its trunk into the heavy-bellied man striding on thick legs, a large creature with broad shoulders, an immense head and sickly yellow face, eyebrows like chewed twigs, the green eyes of a cat poised to gnaw a helpless mouse, a large nose curving to his twisted mouth. Freud heard a hissing from the creature's ragged teeth. The man's unfashionable coat, waistcoat and breeks were gray as ash, yet his stockings were black, shoes adorned with jeweled buckles. His hair stuck out above this gruesome visage like the gray dry leaves of some bush, one hairy fist reached for Freud as if to strangle him. In the other, he held tight a sack of burlap, and things struggled and jolted inside it.

"The optician Coppelius," Nathaniel said in a high-pitched voice, the voice of a young woman beholding her beloved. "The beast who slew my father!" His voice broke, then, and fell in register. Confused, he said, "Or is it my father? Do you live, father?"

Behind the creature, still half hidden in the darkness of the hallway, another waited. It seemed to Freud that he half-recognized that figure. A hand clenched on his heart.

The creature Coppelius seized Nathaniel with one great hairy paw. "Thou didst thyself invite me. For that I must requite thee. Then answer me, then answer me. As my guest, when shall I claim thee?"

Freud surged against his bonds. He cried, "Stand away from the boy. Haven't you done enough harm?"

The young man ignored the alienist, as did his nemesis. "Of fear none shall accuse me. To none will I succumb!"

"Give me your hand!"

"Take it, then! Oh Christ, what deadly chill is this?"

In a kind of nauseated faintness, Freud watched as the creature twisted and removed Nathaniel's hand, then took the other arm and removed that hand as well. It spun the screaming youth about so that he faced Freud, slapped him hard, and with calculated menace loosened the flap of his trews and marched down the flies, unbuttoning each. He flung the garment down to the boy's knees. Freud made a shrill sound. Between the young man's thighs, just as with his sister's, no organs were revealed, only a pale bald curve of unbroken flesh.

"You see? You see?" cried Coppelius. "My handiwork, all mine. So pretty, my dolls. And such pretty eyes!"

He wrapped his great gnarled arms around Nathaniel's chest, from behind, and with all the force of his broad shoulders he jolted the boy's ribcage once, twice, thrice.

The bright blue eyes sprang out of their sockets and rolled, bleeding a little, to Freud's feet.

"Ah, ah," breathed the Olympia doll. Her own eyes were rolled up, white and without pupils, into her sockets.

"Pretty, but used up," Coppelius said in his grating voice. He let Nathaniel's body drop to the floor like a discarded puppet. He moved toward Freud, who shrieked and tried to kick his way free of his bonds. "Come, now, my precious children." The dollmaker foraged in his burlap bag, and out at last scrambled the creatures of the moon, misshapen, hungry, with crooked, snapping beaks. They clambered up Freud's legs, slashing tears in his clothing, and clawed their way toward his bulging eyes. In the darkness of the room, the waiting shape entered finally from the doorway. It was Freud. It took him under the arms and threw him to the floor, then sat, activated the gas lamps, and in the brightening light reached for Freud's casebook, drawing his pen and ink toward it. The things with crooked beaks reached Freud's eyes.

In honor of E.T.A. Hoffmann's "The Sandman"

And Frightened Miss Muffet Away

Paige Quayle

Mother and I are connected by the same liquid marrow with which we spin our webs, webs that traverse the scrub at a height beyond the reach of any beasts of detritus. We are creatures of stealth and balance, instinct and propriety. We communicate by vibration, gesture and sound. Sound, the least important method of communication, is of a frequency that the paneity are unequipped to perceive.

The paneity arrived at a dark period in our history to provide nourishment in time of famine. Their gabbling when caught in our webs, like that of all lower species, is fervent and pointless. Their fanatical gestures serve to further entangle, obscuring them from their fellows on the ground and possible aid. They lack palps and chelicerae and though they have implemented weapons, the paneity are slow in performance. They can't match our speed and their weapons have little effect on the substance of our webs. Their language(s?) are composed of jarring sounds often amplified by tooled devices. They employ few crude gestures and are virtually unintelligible; they often misinterpret each other. They rely on limited vision and hearing and contrived devices that are inadequate for these environs. Everything they do is either futile or disruptive. These deficiencies seal their fate and render them suitable sustenance for a higher race such as ours.

They invaded our world in contrived vehicles that traversed space and/or time, and roam the scrub by means of dual limbs on which they propel themselves across the detritus as crudely as they communicate. They possess two supplemental limbs but these are rarely used for locomotion, never while on the detritus. Whereas, we use all eight limbs fluidly, they're ungainly and inhibited, tottering on two. They house themselves in artificial ground shelters that do not move with detritus winds or quakes, and are poisonous to native leafage. They amass useless possessions, consume unnatural substances that they import (bland liquids and lumps of sour mallow) while they, themselves, are tasty and nutritious. The young ones are juicy and fibrous, an especially pleasing combination. It's a mystery to us why they don't feed on the weak of their own species, as we do. When individuals of the paneity become inert, their companions burn them to ash, a great waste.

Their consistently inept behavior is bewildering. It would seem that creatures with rudimentary language, tools, and social organization would have some intelligence and design intent. But, as well as being physically inefficient, they collect plant and animal life randomly and without purpose, then discard them unutilized; they create burrows, remove minerals, redistribute landmass into awkward configurations that cause flooding, destruction, and sterility. They clutter the middens with their habitation. They're artless. They make a mess.

We take what we need without causing excess disturbance to the scrub. Our webs have a delicate and flexible strength that allows them to move with wind and quake, and not disturb the surrounds. They're an expression of beauty and power that enhance the environs rather than contaminate. They interweave leafage and creature, marry spirit to spirit, bind life to life. Even our excess food is stored neatly in communal bays that blend with the scrub. (The preservative we secrete renders the paneity meat gristly; they're better fresh and frantic).

The paneity have no sensory appendages with which to intuit. They're unable to grasp the meaning of our vibrational sounds and gestures but we have begun to understand some of theirs.

Their sound for us is "rac."

Sometime after the paneity began to appear in large numbers, Mother proposed an experiment. She challenged us to observe the creatures and determine their intent and what other uses they might be put to. The ample ones were consumed, but the mealy were retained for potential application.

The first issue was what to feed them. After spending some time in captivity, they were willing to consume, but were sickened by our insectide. When offered larger wildlife, they accepted gladly but seemed puzzled until one enterprising pan' stripped the skin from an onk, a creature smaller in size but closely resembling the panity. The pan' then removed most of its outer layers. (The panity clad themselves in skins of different species as well as synthetic materials, perhaps they assumed these low creatures did the same.) She gathered what bark and leaves she could reach from her tether, produced a spark and proceeded to burn the meat. Needless to say, our webs do not burn because of the sticky secretions that sustain the compositions and provide secure foothold. The pan' consumed the charred nurture with great relish and tossed bits to fellow creatures within reach. However, the general condition of the panity improved more when fed the feeble liquid and lumps of mallow we obtained from their incompetently fortified stores.

When the captives realized they were not to be eaten or stored as provision, they regained some composure. They initiated sound and gesture directed at us, abet unintelligible. They repeated intonations that were evidently meant to represent themselves. (It seems that each pan' has a slightly different identifying sound for itself as evinced by their interspecies communications, a typically useless complication.) We deciphered some other sounds and gestures but not the reason for the complex system of inefficient communication and behavior they exhibit. We've never deciphered their purpose or what they're compelled to convey. It's assumed they suffered an unfortunate glitch in genetic composition, possibly because of displacement from natal habitat. Even their basic food and procreation particulars are convoluted. Their rate of reproduction, inordinately meager, does not prevail in captivity.

After a period of observation, they were deemed valueless. They're slow moving, weak, and unskillful. They do not adapt to our environs or social order. It was decided that they have no place in scrub or flatlands other than nutriment.

Thus, our population increased dramatically. Our courtship rituals redoubled, transcending all previous revelry. Our offspring grew large, powerful and copious. Silken webbing expanded beyond scrub, extending to flatlands. The elegant and intricate nexus of weave sparkled in light of brilliant daystar and celestial darkness.

In a gesture of benevolence, after diligent scrutiny, I released one pan' captive, the most inventive one, back to the midden where they'd built their main settlement. The frenetic pan' was immediately surrounded by a tumultuous crowd which hushed to her impassioned invocation.

Not long after, a new era commenced.

Rather than increase to our nutritious needs, the paneity flees. New arrivals have ceased; their hives fall to ruin. The uncaptured rabble has escaped via mechanical conveyance and we are confronted with famine once again, obliged to consume local fauna and the weak of our own species. Webs that were once filigree, have devolved to shabby mesh. The marrow that connects me to mother hangs slack.

In honor of Charles Perrault

Richard Nixon Saved From Drowning

Barry N. Malzberg

I

He stares at the window of the Oval Office behind him, thinks: I must not look to see if they are still there. They are gone. They are going. They never appeared at all. Slowly, nonetheless, he turns the chair and looks at the sky then casts his gaze toward the ground on which the crowds jostle and push, wave signs, call soundlessly to one another. Suddenly he is seen in the window. Word passes quickly from one to the other, the crowd shudders as if a wave of feeling had passed through. A wave of feeling for *me* he thinks. They are touched by my condition, they know the extent of my burden. Slowly he raises his hand over his head, moves it in a counterclockwise motion, adjusts his index and third fingers into a V. The Silent Majority shivers in response and waves at him, he waves back to them, they wave at one another in the casting light of his Administration.

II

In grade school, for a little while, he played the violin. The taunting made him give it up but before he took up the piano he had been stubborn about the instrument. He called himself his mother's dog. Trundling to the school, the case dangling from his left hand, he had felt a curious power which fused with shame: he was different, he was better. They could not understand. The Hřímalý exercises had strengthened his right hand so that he could make the V; the mastery of the first position had shown him that the difficulties of the third and fifth positions could be circumvented if he refused to play anything that reached High C.

III

Your enemies, Haldeman said to him, are everywhere. They want you to fail. They need you to fail. Lying in the darkness in the Forbidden City, the exquisite sheets drawn to his neck, Pat sighing or sobbing beside him he had a sudden vision of the Child Emperor returned from antiquity or the grave, leaning over him in the exquisite enclosure of the Royal Chamber. This is your grand opening, your grand opportunity, Haldeman said. Your enemies have identified themselves, they have abandoned secrecy, they stand before you now naked to your forces. We are prepared for the final assault. The Silent Majority have taken their field positions. He had wanted to wander through the surrounding gardens with the Child Emperor, talking of hidden history and his own need to light the fire of alliance but he knew that he could not do this. The Emperor was an illusion, a fabric of dream and excitement and Pat, so sensitive to his movement, would have been disturbed if he had left the bed, found clothing, spoken to a Child Emperor she could not see.

IV

He faces them squarely, heroically meeting their gaze, showing them the face of a hero. People have the right, he says, to know whether their President is a crook. Well, I am not a crook. I earned everything I have. They murmur with approval, shuffle in contrition. And furthermore, he says, they gave me a dog and I am going to keep it. And Pat's good Republican cloth coat. And I am going to continue to fight for what is right. You're my boy, Eisenhower says. He is suspended in the room, vaporous, at enormous height, his childish soon to be Presidential features beaming. That's my boy, Eisenhower says. The ceiling is removed so that he can see the stars. The stars and the cars and the barmen of the great and sweeping land. I herewith declare this mission a success, he says. That must have been a different mission.

V

He seizes absolute power and calls for the bombing runs. Cambodia and Hanoi and Hai Phong Harbor and then Laos. Take out the whole country he says to the joint chiefs. He has never seen Laos but he knows that it is another place like the universities and Hollywood, populated by Communists. And those bastards in London, he says. Drop a load on them too. And Paris. He feels a great rush of vindication; truly purpose, possibility and circumstance have fused. Take them all down, he says. Do you hear that, Henry? I don't have to take this any more. Fifth position had been a mystery. How could you put the first finger on High C and stay in tune? The distance between notes became so small. Don't worry about it, Isaac Stern said decades later when he asked him. Above the third position it's all guesswork anyway. You play by ear. He dreams that he is on a Christmas run over the Gulf of Tonkin, just he and the bombardier. Take us down, he says. I want to see the water.

VI

He had left Dallas, was already aloft when he heard the news. It did not surprise him. The Kennedys had always walked on the edge of death, eaten at the table disaster. Their authority came from their seeming indifference to death. They were not the enemy but they *were* the enemy; they moved almost casually in and then out of their danger and at the end, coming into November in 1960 he felt himself overwhelmed by a knowledge he could no longer suppress: he was going to lose because they could lie better than he. Somewhere in his most inner heart he was possessed of a truth to which Kennedy was indifferent; the truth was one of insufficiency. How could you play above the Fifth Position? It was all fakery and instinct. But Kennedy would not even acknowledge that; to Kennedy fakery and rigor were interchangeable. They were exactly the same. You were one, then you were the other. No one knew and no one cared. They only knew that Kennedy was beautiful. All of the Kennedys were beautiful. The men fucked anyone they wanted anywhere they wanted and the women were happy to go along with all of that because the old man carried a checkbook everywhere. Whereas he had had to carry that damned violin into the classroom, he had had to carry water for Eisenhower for years while never getting more than a handshake. What contributions has he made to your Administration? Well, if you give me a few days, maybe I can think of one.

VII

Hunter Thompson had somehow gotten into the limousine with him. Just a quick interview on the way to the airport. Throw it, Thompson had shouted at him in the parking lot, Throw the big one Dick. Big strapping guy, thought he was so clever, thought that he was the leader of the hippies and the derelicts, just another godamned reporter with big plans but he was covering the campaign for Rolling Stone so you had to pay attention, had to be nice. Otherwise he would kill you on paper and even though no one who mattered read Rolling Stone, he knew the garbage national press and wires would pick up some of Thompson's lines and run them. That was the trouble, they were everywhere, enemies were in every pocket of the nation and even though they made a joke of the Enemies List, where the hell would the country have been if Hiss had had his way? If the Hollywood Ten had had their way? If they hadn't gone out with Chambers and *gotten* that evidence. The country would have sunk in their lies and corruption. Tell that to Hunter Thompson, tell that to the hippies and monsters at Rolling Stone: You were the USA I saved from drowning.

VIII

He finds himself in pounding California surf, still in suit jacket and tie, with pant cuffs rolled, trying to return to the shore but the waters are insistent, they overwhelm his ankles and then his knees and he sways, loses balance, topples to the damp, gritty sand. He waits for help, waits to be pulled from this sudden scrambling darkness but even as he flails feels nothing but the water. In the shocking, overwhelming influx he holds the damp sands and waits, waits for the hands of rescue, waits for ascension from the darkness, waits for the fuming, casting, casual and finally exhilarating light.

The Terminal Villa

Barry N. Malzberg

"And in the epilogue, Mr. Cheney writes that after undergoing heart surgery in 2010, he was unconscious for weeks. During that period, he wrote, he had a prolonged, vivid dream that he was living in an Italian villa, pacing the stone paths to get coffee and newspapers."

– *The New York Times*, 8/25/11

ONE

Afterward, in the strange and pungent mists of transit, Cheney thought he could remember the serving girl, remember those stressed limbs, the battered face, the enlarging and translucent angle of her regard as she paced the stone paths of the villa, bringing him coffee and newspapers. His own hands trembled with necessity as he reached toward her, then away, the contact too glancing through the passed objects to grant him the fusion which he desperately needed. Her eyes were wide in the perpetual daylight, soft with knowledge but also hard with embitterment and he felt that if he could but touch her cheekbones, feel the planes of her face, those eyes would meet his in a gaze more insistent than the thunder of the birds plummeting between the trees and stone monuments of the villa.

TWO

Cheney felt that he could see beyond her, could see beyond the trees and the yellowcake uranium which littered the grounds to the very heart of the ruined country. Angled through the intersections of the paths were, Cheney could imagine, dwarfish and half-hidden enemy forces, forces which had carried the yellowcake at some earlier time to this difficult proximity and who were observing him, chattering in code, reporting his movements. Cheney remembered a time when the yellowcake had been fresh and new, had not been carried by dwarves to the villa, a time when the yellowcake like the nuclear ordnance itself had laid deep in the corrupt and sprawling Iraquian tablelands. That had been at a time when Cheney, then untrammeled by age and his terrible knowledge, had had other priorities, priorities which had ordered and made clean his life. That had been a time of clarity, a time before dwarves and yellowcake and the stone paths of the villa which he trod endlessly and restlessly, prowled like a disease, in search of the woman who brought him the coffee and the newspapers.

THREE

Sometime later, past events which in the busy glare of yellowcake and fire he could not truly recollect, Cheney dreamed of the times that he had managed to lay with the woman, had first carried her beyond the stoned paths to a forested and secret cavern where he had been able to work his climactic will upon her. In these dreams beyond the villa it was not Italy but Iraq in which they lay, whispering terrific secrets to one another in the soft glow of nuclear celebration. "You were always my priority," Cheney dreamed he whispered and felt himself trembling like a Wyoming sunset, in that diminished fire he suddenly thought it possible then that he had merged with her as he had with Iraq, as he had with the secrecy of the villa, the secrecy of the extracted plans, just he and she now in profound and subtle embrace, just the two of them and the yellowcake and the memory of dwarves and fire.

In honor of J.G. Ballard

H. P. Lovecraft

The Doom that Came to Devil's Reef

Don Webb

For Michel Houellebecq

Among Lovecraft's papers at Brown University was a large manila envelope containing a school exercise notebook and a newspaper clipping. The notebook's owner Miss Julia Phillips had been mistakenly identified as a cousin of American horror writer Howard Phillips Lovecraft (1890-1937). Over four-fifth's of the pen and pencil entries are rather commonplace detailing Miss Phillips life as a seamstress in the Providence of the 1920s, her growing depression and her commitment to Butler Hospital. As both of Lovecraft's parents had ended their years in the selfsame institution, Julia had been perceived as another branch of a less than mentally healthy tree. It wasn't until Lovecraft's biographer S. T. Joshi read the volume that it was seen as anything other than a rather dreary memento. It is in the last few pages of the book wherein Julia's dreams or waking fancies take an amazingly cosmic tone that the book became of interest to Lovecraftian scholars. The relationship of Julia and Howard is unknown. Lovecraft had little interest in psychiatry, rather than his occasionally denunciation of Freud in his letters. No one has been able to discover how Lovecraft came into possession of the book.

What is clear is that Julia's fantasies became Lovecraft's inspiration for his 1932 novella "The Shadow Over Innsmouth." Lovecraft's notes in the volume are slight, but he occasionally erased Julia's words altogether and wrote in his fictional equivalents. For example Julia records that she is writing about the real world Massachusetts town of Newburyport where Julia had spent her childhood. Lovecraft erased all but one incident of "Newburyport" and wrote in "Innsmouth." Likewise certain demons or gods of Julia's delusions have been replaced with Cthulhu, Dagon and Mother Hydra. It is tempting to speculate that Lovecraft had considered the diary as a sort of *objet trouvé* or readymade to continue the mythic patterns that he begun in earlier work especially "The Call of Cthulhu" (1926). Perhaps Julia's rather simple style, reflecting her fifth grade education, was too limiting for Lovecraft, or perhaps the whole notion struck him as artistically dishonest. Given Lovecraft's penchant for recording even the smallest details of his moods and life in his letters it seems remarkable that Julia's diary was never mentioned.

Inevitably that class of literalist thinker that assumes that all of Lovecraft's stories are some sort of mystic channelings, have claimed that the diary of Julia Phillips is the work of a kindred soul – likewise expressing the "mysteries of the Aeon." Perhaps Lovecraft himself, who had played with the artistic notion of art and dream coming from sort of Otherness, was attracted to and then repulsed by the contents of this diary for that seeming. Again unless further documentation comes to light we shall never know. Here is what we do know about Julia Phillips. She was the third of six children to be born to Rodger Allen and Susan Williams Phillips. Born in 1891, she was a year younger than Lovecraft. Her father was a green grocer and her mother supplemented the family's income with sewing, a skill young Julia excelled at. Her sickly youth kept her a homebody while her two brothers joined the merchant marine and her three better-adjusted (an apparently better-looking) sisters found husbands. When her parents died she went to live with her eldest sister Velma and alternated between manic periods of religiosity and depressed periods of terrible lethargy. At first she was the merely eccentric aunt, whose finical contribution was greatly valued. As time wore in, she became worrisome to her sister and brother-in-law. In 1924 Julia tried to kill herself with rat poison after months of the darkest depression. The family had her committed to Butler. She remained in Butler until 1927. For the majority of her stay she was a model patient. She repaired the garments of other patients, took part in the sing-alongs and greeted her family in a sane and cheery tone during their infrequent visits. The entries prior to her commitment were made in pen, the hospital only allowed a No.1 pencil during Julia's stay.

The last dated entry in Julia's diary was August 7, the day the "Peace Bridge" was opened between Fort Erie, Ontario and Buffalo, New York – "perhaps mankind has learned to live in Peace – God bless Prince Edward and Prince Albert and Governor Smith." In late August 1927 Julia began obsessing on a hurricane that hit the Atlantic shore of Canada. She complained that authorities were unaware of the danger the sea stood for. She warned (somewhat prophetically) of an upcoming Pacific earthquake. In early September most of her freedoms of movement in the hospital grounds were curtailed when she either shaved off or otherwise removed most of her hair. It was at this time Julia did involve herself in what limited art therapy the Butler offered. She painted five canvasses of "disturbing maritime scenes." These seem to have been sold at the annual art show, sadly little is know of them save that they used the (at that time) radical technique of grattage, which had been introduced to the art world by Max Ernst. Exactly how an undereducated American woman would invent the same art technique that a German surrealist had created for his series of paintings of "enchantment and terror," is more than a bit of a mystery. Perhaps the art instructor had kept abreast of the European art scene. It is likely that during this time, the "channeled" portion of the diary was written.

On September 14, an underwater earthquake in Japan killed 108 people. The next day a "Mr. Kenneth S. Gilman" paid a visit to Miss Julia. All of Miss Julia's visitors had been either been family of former sewing clients, and it was assumed that he belonged in these categories. He paid three visits and winning the confidence of the staff took Julia on a carriage ride. They never returned. The newspaper treated it as a major crisis – for two days. A legal notice of her being declared dead appeared seven years later, three years after that Lovecraft died of intestinal cancer. Mr. Joshi suggests that Lovecraft, having taken an interest in the case because of the two articles in the *Brown Daily Herald* had contacted the director of the institution. Perhaps a lack of interest or sense of shame on the part of Julia's family had made them uninterested in the notebook. Perhaps the notebook had merely been lent to Lovecraft and he failed to return it

In addition to the change of narrative voice in the last section of the diary, the handwriting becomes bolder. Some of the margins are decorated with little glyphs of stylized fish reminiscent of the Rongorongo glyphs if Easter Island. The theology and cosmology of the piece seem to be a mixture of native Australian religion and a good deal of Lovecraftian musings. Since Julia's background would seem to suggest no clear method of knowing the former, and *Weird Tales* an unlikely reading material for Butler Hospital – the passages are striking.

Here are the final words of Julia Phillips, where Lovecraft has erased her words and written in his own we will indicate with *italics*:

In the changeable world of land something dire is happening. The humans are learning to kill themselves, which is good I think, and learning to kill the seas, which would mean death to the world. The seas taste of their oil and trash. The beautiful mother of pearl walls of our new home *Devil's Reef* is stained black. I hate this place, the waters are much too cold, and the fishing is poor. Our new home has no name, the Great *Cthulhu* has not dreamed of it yet. We had great hopes as He reached out to us and our weakened descendants the humans two orbits ago. He tries to bring Thought to all life here, that is why He came to this watery globe from the green star in my great-great grandmother's time. He is such a suffering god. The humans have re-cast Him as one of their own. They think He brings salvation instead of Thought. All will think here even the plants and the fungi if the humans do not hurt the water too much. He rose briefly two orbits ago. He will stir in a few days, but not rise. We have learned how he tosses and turns. I am not hopeful for the humans, they are too degenerate from us. Even those we have crossbred with can live only a few hundred orbits. No wonder they kill this world; they do not stay here long enough to love it. It seems wrong to me to bring self awareness to such a species.

The hope of Ra-natha-alene to save the human race by intermarrying with them is not held by many of us. It did not work in my youth and it does not work now. The humans are greedy for gold so it was easy to make a deal with *Marsh* but they do not profit by our Teaching. In the spiral towers of their cells we help them find the way back, we make them more beautiful, but it is not enough. On the land they hide away when their Beauty starts to show. They wear our crowns, but they do not Think, or if they Think it is as something minor – an artist or a magician. No architects. No mathematicians. No biologists.

There was a storm recently, much cold water was disturbed to the north of our new home. We had not controlled it by Dreaming. It is not in the Dreamtime and the hateful aurora wind from space keeps Deep Thoughts from hatching in our brains. The storm affected me badly, scattering some of my mind into human bodies. I will have to gather myself together. I hate their world with its right angles that turn thinking into sleeping. There were deaths in Canada, a cold white land. Not enough deaths I think.

The humans of *Innsmouth* have learned a little about Dreaming in their Swirl, they spill blood and sexual fluids to *Father Dagon and Mother Hydra*, but they think in animal terms, they are too much of the life of this world. They have taken the animal needs and called them Sex and Money. Even when they become Beautiful, theses two abstractions rule them. I am worried that they will subvert our goals. Some among them believe that warm-blooded animals are evolved – more progressive than we. The humans worship themselves though a demon called Darwin. If their line of faith were right I would be greater than my grandmother, my grandmother would be greater than hers, and she would be greater than *Mother Hydra*. Yet a few of the humans have discovered entropy. A few know the cosmos is decaying.

Bad news has come from the *Esoteric Order of Dagon* the humans of North America have spread the bloodlines beyond Ra-natha-alene's plan. They know that when the Change comes upon humans they will seek us out. Therefore they reason that humans changing will move back to Newburyport and bring wealth and connections from their lives with them. They seek to intermarry with traveling salesmen in a ridiculous scheme to make their town more of a center of commerce. They don't care how this can spread out tendrils of our souls. Their belief that each being has a unique soul leads to the simple numerical argument of more of "Us" equals more power. In orbits of bad sunspot activity (such as this year) the changing humans will Dream of us, or will have parts of the Dreamtime of Great *Cthulhu* become parts of their foundational consciousness. They don't understand what a strain their Change places upon us. Each new hybrid pulls at our peace, especially in place not established by the Dreamtime. . Soon such humans will come to *Innsmouth* and we will literally be pulled to the land to greet them, our nurturing instincts taking the place of our common sense. Worse still humans, who have not heard the Dream cantrips when they eat their mother's slime will know great fear. They will see their Change in terms of death, not rebirth. And as they are not conscious entities they cannot think directly of death. Death to a being that can not remember anything before its hatching is a terrible consciousness. In the myths of the humans they dimly know they were deathless. But they see this as some sort of garden. One of the hybrid offspring in Florida is trying to recreate the Dreamtime there just as the people of Nan Madol did a few hundred orbits ago. Ra-natha-alene thinks these stirrings of true Architecture might trigger some ancestral memories on the human's part, but I am dubious. Some of us are having glimpses of human minds during the daytime.

I have seen myself trapped in a body with disgustingly scaleless skin and hair. I fear that I will Dream myself there pushed by the aurora.

I will dance at the Council and try to persuade the mothers to leave this place and swim back to our second home. We must regroup where the architecture is strong, and Dreams are caught and farmed and milked in the old way. We must prepare against the human onslaught. Once our race was mighty. Were we not the race that called the dolphins and whales back to the sea? Were we not the race that broke up the single large landmass, or kept the ages of ice at bay? If only we had not experimented with the hairy ones adding to their spirals. What arrogance seeking to bring self-awareness to this dying world. The humans inherited our arrogance but not our wisdom. They see us as their dry-land ancestors living in lands that have sunken – Atlantis, Lemuria, *Rlyeh*. As they degenerate their myths will say we lost our footing due to black magic. They can't even guess that our life cycle is hampered by their yellow sun's deadly radiation. If we last until that star is normal and the great bands of radiation leave this world, we will flourish again. Let us wait, I shall dance to the mothers, let us wait until the stars are right. Then we can Gift the creatures of this world with Dreamtime. Ra-natha-alene and her sisters mock me. They say that humans cannot grow to be a threat. They ignore the vast expansion of human numbers in the time since Nan Madol. They argue that as Great *Cthulhu* makes human artists and mystics Dream, humans will give up their fixation with death. No race can kill a planet they say. I warn them, there is no race as vile as humans.

Worse news has come. The hybrids came to *Devil's Reef* to swim and Dance at the new moon. One of the wandering rogue offspring has come to *Innsmouth*. He does not know that he is of us. His instincts provoke him to actions and accidents that he sees as chance. He is the hotel. The mothers grew excited, their gill slits flaring purple. They will rise and seek him out. I see that this will lead to disaster. They will seek to nurture and protect him. What will happen if he merely flees them? They cannot kill one of their children even if his blood is nauseatingly warm and his skin covered in hair. It could take only one revealing our presence to harm us here. There is no Dreamtime in the walls of our new home. Humans have grown deadly, yet the mothers do not believe what the Spiral has told us of their war in Europe.

It has happened, as I feared. The nursery parade gathered in town last night and the human saw them and heard the croaking of the nursery songs. The sounds released the Change, but he had not been fed the Dreams as the *Innsmouth* children had been. Even though I loathe humans, I felt pity for this long-lost cousin. I can imagine the rapid beating of his heart. I can imagine the cooling of his blood, which to him would feel like death. The great Priestesses had put on their tiaras and the hybrid Priestesses had put on the robes. They made their slow awkward way toward his room. It was easy for him to outrun them. Without the Dreamtime to guide him he would have seen this all as nightmare.

With luck his shock will silence him before he can tell others, and then when the Change comes upon him, he will seek us out. His skin will grow scaly and only the soothing feel of salt water will bring relief. His nascent gills will swell, and our thoughts will be drawn to his head like the bees of his world are drawn to blooming flowers. The Beauty will overcome terror. Tonight I will pray and Dance at the thrones of my ancestors *Father Dagon and Mother Hydra.* May they soothe his mind and still his lips! May his Change not bring fear!

There have been Navy ships over our reef the last two days. We try to send them Dreams, but the steel hulls of the ships reflect our wills back to us. It is as I feared. It is not like the old orbits, when we touched their minds and they saw mermaids calling each to each. They mothers said the words of light and made the wheels of bioluminescence appear in the water, vast whirling signs. But this did not soothe the humans. Once humans have weapons they are not willing to be soothed, so far have they degenerated from us.

Canisters began to fall from the sides of the ships, half our size. I began swimming. They were depth charges and they exploded with epic sound against our reef. The walls of our new home shattered, great panes of mother of pearl began wheeling through the water, reflecting the lights of the bioluminescent wheels and the explosions filling the sea with green and pink lightning. Shock wave after shockwave passed though the ocean – and dead and dying fish buffeted my body as I swam with all my might. Then some jagged pieces of the mother of pearl began to cut into me and my dark blood mixed crazily with the glowing waters. I felt the drums of my ears pop and the violent storm around me became strangely still. More of the fragments tore into me. I saw the arms of my mother floating by leaving a wake of dark pupil blood and the smell of raw death. I prayed to *Mother Hydra* that she may Sleep and Dream until her next Cycle. I reached out for her soul and found nothing but the cold unforgiving water. Then a fragment of shell struck my face and I was cut free from my body. I tried to make my soul Sleep with the words that bring Sleep: Fhtagn nerzin kyron Meftmir!

I did not Sleep but was sucked into the mind of a human, the one I had glimpsed before. A female that has not made the slime of motherhood. She was confined in a place of the mad, where the smells are terrible and the light is harsh. She is made to listen to a horrible caterwauling called hymns, and to eat dead food and be treated with metabolic poisons superstitiously thought to calm her mind. Fortunately her mind is strong, so strong that she had never been able to fit into their world. She was born in *Innsmouth* several orbits ago. She is one of the rogue lines, descendant from *Marsh* himself four generations ago. She was not brought up in our way, but as a human and thinks that the divine would be found in her terrible form.

I hate the way the air does not support her ugly body as she walks about. I try to Remember who I am by writing and painting. I tried once to Dance, but the other humans restrained the body. For days they kept me from moving. I cannot believe that they could be so cruel. I wished to kill the body and try again to Sleep, but the humans worship bodies and will not let me do so.

In the past few days I have found ironic hope. I cannot send my soul far, so I know not what lies on the far side of the world. Yet I have no reason to presume that our Pacific home has fallen. Surely the strange angles of the Dreamtime have kept the Watery Abyss intact! But I found him. The one who brought the doom to *Devil's Reef*. With the cruel irony of this planet, the Change came upon him the day of the depth charges. His body yearned for the sea just as our new home was pounded to flinders. I am nurturing him. As a true being I was not old enough to be a mother, but in this human body I can make the slime and feel the emotions. I enveloped him with the love of the mother.

We have made a plan. He will come to this place and free me. He understands the human world well. He has done certain things to his appearance to hide the Change. He will spirit my body away. He tells me that this will be easy because humans do not value females and mad females are of no use. He has enough money to buy us train tickets to the West Coast. He will take me to a place with the lovely name of Land's

End and there we will shed both human clothes and form. I feel that I can awaken the sea form of this Julia. We will swim to our home and dwell there in glory.

Thus ends the words of Julia Phillips' diary. The only other item in Lovecraft's envelope was a clipping from the *Brown Daily Herald* describing the testing of a new depth charge on Ward's Reef near Newburyport. The bombing went on for three days . . .

In honor of Lovecraft

Five Fingers

Gary Lovisi

For decades I had been obsessed with the little known, supernatural conundrum I'd dubbed "The Borlsover Affair". I'd heard and read snatches of it here and there of course, but never beheld the truth of the matter until now.

The story particularly intrigued me as I was a writer — one who can only create his stories in original first draft by hand — hence I became obsessed with the tale of an animated appendage told to me by one of the survivors of the affair. The man was named Saunders — an old and rather unsavory broken fellow living out his last days as a mathematical master at a second-rate suburban school. Upon the application of a far too liberal mixture of alcoholic beverages one evening I forced him to tell me the entire tale — a grotesque nightmarish story he had often intimated to me, but never fully told, for the fear was always upon him. The alcohol loosened his tongue as I knew it would that dark late October night, before Halloween would come upon us, as he told me the full tale of the Borlsover Family. He began recounting the sad life of old cantankerous Adrian Borlsover, gone blind but gifted with some form of automatic writing in his animated right hand, and of his young nephew, Eustace — and then of the hand itself.

"A beast with five fingers it was, Mr. Jameson," Saunders grimly whispered to me in the dark corner of a secluded booth in an empty barroom that chilly evening. "Not a proper hand at all was it. Long bony fingers, muscle to it certainly, but no warm flesh nor blood. A demon thing, haunted by some disembodied spirit of Adrian Borlsover or some other of the Borlsover clan — a human hand that put pen to paper to write such blasphemy as one could never imagine. I think the entire family was cursed. Poor Eustace! The hand took him eventually."

I nodded grimly, for I believed the man entirely. I believed him because over the many years of research and through vast expense, I now had the hand in my possession, locked away in a safe in my home.

I told this all to Saunders. His eyes bugged wide in terror, froth flecking at his lips as he appeared momentarily unable to utter any words.

"So will you help me?" I asked him plainly, impatiently. My plan was to investigate the hand, understand it, to control it, and Saunders was the one man alive who possessed that knowledge. He was someone who had actual experience with the thing and could help me make it do my bidding. Long ago, Eustace Borlsover and he had discovered it, on that dark day a mysterious small box was delivered to Eustace with his uncle's severed right hand inside it.

Saunders shook, took a long drink. "You have it, don't you? You son of a bitch! Why? Why on Earth! How ever did you find it?"

"It was not easy, Mr. Saunders, I can assure you. The time and expense was excessive but... Well, who can place a value upon such a thing? I am a writer, as I told you before, and I write all my work by hand with pen on paper — in the classic style. It is the only way I can write and I make a very successful living from it. All first drafts are done in that manner, then after editing I transpose the manuscript to my computer for further rewriting and editing, but the idea phase — that most important part of the creative process — I can only do by hand with pen to paper first."

"Automatic writing?" he asked with a wild-eyed look of suspicion.

"Perhaps...?" I replied softly. "I imagine one might call it that if one were to think in those terms. The mind creates the ideas, but the hand holding the pen writes them all down carefully and with great speed. Writing them faster than I could ever type them. Better than I could ever speak them into any recording device. While each writer has their own system that works best for them, this is the only way I can create my work."

"But sometimes, doesn't it seem to you that the hand writes what it will, almost with a mind of its own?" Saunders asked hoarsely.

"Yes, it does," I replied with a sly grin. "Sometimes in the heat of the creative process...the hand seems to do what it will."

"So what is it you want?"

I laughed at him, then smiled indulgently, "Mr. Saunders, I know not what you are thinking. My success enables me to indulge myself in these little conundrums that I find interesting, fascinating, even exhilarating. The story of the hand of Adrian Borlsover is one I have been obsessed with for a long time, and now I own the thing."

"You may think *you* own it, Mr. Jameson," Saunders husked dryly, trying to hold back the evident terror he felt lodged within from long dark memories, "but I am afraid that it owns *you* now as well."

"Nonsense," I said briskly, impatient, refusing to accommodate the fearfulness and abject blue funk that had overtaken him. "I want to study the thing and more so — what I really want to do is set it to writing for me, then to read what mysterious words and sentences it will put down on paper. Who knows what mysteries it will unlock and tell us?"

Saunders looked at me with utter disbelief. "It is a demon haunted thing and no good can ever come of its use. I would fear its words, sir, I would fear the print from a pen written by such a hand."

"Not I! I should be delighted to read what it has to write down for us, Mr. Saunders," I told him firmly. "Come now, join me in this endeavor and I can assure you, you never need want for money. I know you are perpetually short on funds, but if you join me you need never fear that situation again."

"Aye, I am low on funds but I fear not poverty — I drink up most of my pay to keep the nightmare's away — for it is an old fear that rattles around in my bones about that hand, Mr. Jameson. I still see it in my mind's eye, scurrying across the floor of Master Eustace's library, climbing up the drapes, cater pillaring its long bony fingers along the book shelves. It's a nightmare I'll never forget, but I will join you and help you as best I am able, just as I did young Eustace, God rest his soul. But not only for money will I do this work, but upon your command I will be there to destroy the creature when you come to your senses to allow it to be done."

I laughed heartily at that, "I don't think that will ever happen, Mr. Saunders. But I accept your service and will pay you well for your advice and experience. Now let us get home and get some sleep, for we start our adventure bright and early tomorrow morning promptly at eight am."

I helped Saunders to a cab that took him to his run-down hovel of an apartment. Then I drove to my townhouse, my mind swirling with thoughts of what marvelous words that amazing hand would soon put to paper for me.

The next day promptly at eight am, Jenkins, my assistant, let Mr. Saunders into my parlor for our initial meeting. I must say that for the amount of drink, lack of sleep, and his advanced age, he seemed remarkably sharp and alert.

"I'm here, Mr. Jameson, I'm ready to begin," he stated firmly, though I thought my eyes could detect a slight tremor of his left hand. Tension, fear, terror, or early onset of some debilitating disease? I did not know, nor did I much care, for we had important work to do.

"Then let us get started," I said, leading him into my large wood-paneled book-lined study and closing the door resoundingly behind me. "We are alone now."

Saunders looked in awe around my large library, which was the pride of my home. High shelves along all four walls full with books rose almost 20 feet in height, topped off by a large glass skylight in the center of the room. "By God, the place reminds me of old Adrian Brolsover's library. That was a foul place of dark happenings and dire memories."

I smiled ignoring his grim words. Instead I said, "It is time we begin our work. I suppose you would like to examine the hand first?"

Saunders blanched, "It's here! In this very room!"

"Yes, in this very room, I have it locked away in my safe."

Saunders gulped nervously, "Young Master Eustace once locked the hand away in a safe — and it got out."

"Fear not, Saunders, all is secure here," I told him briskly. I would have offered the poor sot a drink but I feared that at the moment he was unnerved quite enough. Better to calm him and show him that the hand posed us no threat.

I undid the combination of my safe and brought out a cigar-box sized wooden case and placed it on my desk in front of us. There was a bolt lock that secured the lid and I instantly undid it.

Saunders gasped in terror, and I couldn't help but let out a slight laugh. "It is quite safe, Saunders, I assure you."

Then I opened the lid and we beheld the hand. It was the severed, dried, blackened, long fingered right hand of Adrian Borlsover. There was a deep indentation in it where Saunders had told me it had been nailed to a board by Eustace long ago. There was no board, nor nail now, and the hand lay there entirely still and unmoving — a horrible severed human appendage!

"It really is quite harmless. In fact, I must admit it rather disappoints me," I told Saunders, who looked upon the thing mouth agape. I continued, "With all I had heard and read about it, I expected some movement, some form of life or animation of the fingers, something — but in all the days I have possessed it, it has not made one single movement."

"Be thankful of that, Mr. Jameson."

I laughed, "Well, regardless, here it is. It is not doing anything, and we can examine it to our heart's content. Would you like a drink?"

Saunders nodded absently, his eyes could not leave the hand, "I could sure use one, sir."

"Very well," I called in Jenkins and told my man to bring us two bourbons — Saunders and I had been imbibing the very same the previous evening so I assumed that would be acceptable to him, and he agreed.

I covered the hand with my handkerchief once Jenkins appeared to take our order, then uncovered it once he'd brought our drinks and left the room. The hand was still there, of course, apparently having not moved at all.

Saunders was shivering by now. He lunged for his glass and downed the dark fluid with relief or terror — who could truly say.

I sipped my drink slowly as I looked carefully at the motionless hand.

"And it has not moved since you first obtained it?" Saunders asked curious, somewhat hopeful, to my dismay.

"Not one iota."

He nodded, looked down at the hand laying there upon the top of my desk, "And how long has it been in your possession?"

"One week, and I have examined it carefully each and every day. I must admit I am disappointed that the thing seems dead, unmoving. How can it write anything if it can not even move?"

"Is that so important to you? That it take up a pen and write?" Saunders asked me, calmer now, but with serious concern in his voice.

"Of course! I am a writer. I am fascinated to see what words it will put to paper, but there is something else…"

Saunders looked at me now with dark suspicion in his eyes. I just laughed, "My dear fellow, it is not that bad, I assure you. Look at my hands, especially my right hand which I use for my writing."

"Arthritis?"

"Yes, rather severe and growing worse," I told him with a sigh. "Soon my very means of earning a living — a quite nice moneyed living by the way — will end. For if I can not write using my hand to hold pen to paper, I am doomed."

"But surely you can use a typewriter? Or one of those new computers, or even hire a secretary…?"

"For editing and copy certainly, but not for the creative process. No, none of that will work for me. I have tried everything. The creative process is a complex and delicate one, one's muse can be a fickle bitch at times. I am only able to write by hand and now my livelihood will be ruined. I must find a way to make the hand responsive to my commands. I know it can be done."

"That you shall never do, Mr. Jameson. The thing has a mind — if one can say such — of its own. It is not the mind of Adrian Borlsover, whom I knew, but something else, something quite malevolent. If I were you I would douse it with gasoline and set it ablaze right away. Destroy it before it destroys you. It is of no use to you as it is, so why not dispose of it here and now? I will help you do it. Please."

"Nonsense! Look, Saunders, I hired you because you have experience with the thing, with trapping it and controlling it. I want you to get it working for me. I want it moving and writing again!"

"You're quite mad, you know that."

"But I pay well, eh, Saunders?"

"You pay well, and I'll do it, but not only for the money."

Saunders and I worked on various plans to reanimate the hand. After we each examined it minutely, we were convinced that it was dead. I decided it needed to be shocked into wakefulness. Saunders vehemently disagreed with this idea but I overruled him. I began by using sharp probes, long pins and needles, to poke and prod the thing, but it was all to no avail. Old Saunders was shocked by my actions and warned of reprisals, but I heeded him not. Then I came upon the idea of using a battery to give the thing an electric shock.

"A good jolt of electricity may just do the trick, eh, Saunders?" I asked, setting up the apparatus. I first tried a 9 volt battery, but when there was no reaction, I grew more ambitious and set it up using a far larger automobile battery. The connection instantly caused the hand fly off my desk and fall to the floor. Lifeless and motionless. It was hot and smoking as I picked it up and replaced it upon my desk. Saunders was mumbling to himself by then, but I could not make out his words.

I was severely disappointed, depressed even, for nothing we tried seemed to reanimate the hand. I had spent so much money and many years of my life to procure this now useless object that my frustration boiled over in sudden rage. I attacked the hand with a knife, stabbing it repeatedly as I cursed it and all the Borlsovers I could think of. I shouted vile words as I plunged the knife into it again and again.

"Stop!" Saunders ordered, finally restraining me. "What are you doing! You'll make it — mad!"

"Good, then if it has any feelings, any life left in it at all, it should get mad. By God, I'll give the damn thing something to get mad about!"

"No, don't do it!"

I pushed old Saunders aside and continued to stab away viciously into the dried up blackened thing, my knife cutting deep gouges into it — and through it — the knife going into the wood of my desktop. The hand gave off no reaction. None at all. There was muscle tissue there, bone and sinew, but no warmth, and no flesh or blood at all.

I grew despondent, my writing career was over and the fortune I had spent to obtain the hand had been wasted. I was in debt and broke. With a curse I hurled the useless thing across the room where it smacked against a bookcase. It dropped to the floor with a dull thud. *Then the thing moved.* The fingers twitched, and quickly in the manner of a geometer caterpillar, the fingers humped up one moment, flattened the next, the thumb appeared to give it a crablike motion, and the hand righted itself upon it's fingertips and quickly shot off behind the bookcase. It was gone in an instant.

I was astounded and looked at Saunders. He was cringing in terror.

"You've done it now!" he whispered in dire warning.

"Did you see that, Saunders?" I barked, seeking his verification. Verification that I had not imagined what I had just seen, nor gone entirely mad. Insane.

"You've done it now, Master Jameson," was all he said in an accusing tone, adding fearfully, "Now you've made it mad. Master Eustace made it mad and no good can come of it now."

I swallowed hard, it was a lot to get used to. Not the fact that the hand might be mad at me, that was pure poppycock, but that it had indeed moved! That it had actually come to life! This was wonderful!

"Come on, Saunders," I blurted full of excitement. "We must trap it!"

"Aye, now we must, but we shall not."

"Oh, come now, it's just a thing, only a hand, nothing more. We can trap it and then I can use it for my own ends."

Well, I uttered those words to Saunders days ago with utmost confidence, but they had not proved true. The thing possessed an uncanny energy and wiliness I never would have thought possible. It hid from us and was difficult to find. Every time Saunders and I would seem to trap it, it escaped our grasp.

I locked down my library, we nailed shut the windows,

boarded up all vents, bolted the door. I gave Jenkins strict orders never to enter the room unless by a prearranged signal. I did not want the thing to get loose and escape. I felt sure that while we had it locked within my library it was just a matter of time before we would find it and capture it.

Saunders and I never left the library now except to bring in items for use to trap the thing, which all eventually failed. We slept in the library on cots, taking turns keeping watch. We tried many ways to find the thing and trap it but nothing worked. It was as if it were playing some game with us, hiding out just to spite us. Though none of our plans had worked as of yet, I knew I would eventually capture that hand and I would not let anything stop me.

It was on the night before Halloween when the moon was full, beams of illumination coming in through the library skylight, when I saw the hand. It was upright upon fingertips, slowly walking along the top rail of a high bookshelf. I could plainly see its' silhouette against the skylight. I dared not move for fear of alerting it. Saunders was fast asleep in his cot — as it was my watch just then. I reasoned that to awaken him might alert the hand to hide itself, so I did my best to be quiet and began to stalk the thing.

Silently I moved closer and quietly climbed the mobile library stairway I used to reach the upper shelves. The hand was motionless now, I could see it plainly against the skylight glass. It seemed to be transfixed by the light from the full moon. I moved up the steps. Quietly. Silently. I had just a few more steps to go and I would be even with it — close enough to quickly grasp it into my hands. I knew I could do this, I could surprise the thing and capture it in one feel swoop. I took the last step, the wooden ladder beneath my foot gave the slightest creek. I shuddered in fear that the sound had given me away, but the hand remained motionless. I was almost upon it. I reached over and outstretched my fingers to grasp the hand, when it suddenly turned and flung itself off the shelf upon me. It's long cold bony fingers instantly grasped my throat and closed tightly. I gasped, I could not breath. I was flung back by the surprise of the attack and had to do my damnedest using my left hand to hold onto the ladder so as not to fall the 20 feet to the library floor below. My right hand vainly tried to pry the thing's fingers from my throat, as I desperately tried to breathe.

By then the ruckus had woken Saunders. "Mr. Jameson?" I heard him ask in alarm. Then he looked up and must have seen us struggling there at the top of the ladder against the skylight and the full moon. He saw me and shouted, "Mr. Jameson! I told you it would come to no good!"

I barely heard his words for I was in a life and death struggle with a demon thing that possessed supernatural strength I had never encountered before. I gasped for breath, my eyes bugging as I struggled to keep my balance on the ladder. I tried to pry the creature's fingers from my throat but it was to no avail. They were like steel rods. I was gurgling froth, then blood. Finally I could hold onto the ladder no longer, I felt myself losing consciousness and tried to scream — the scream stifled in my throat by the tightening pressure of the demon hand.

Then I lost my grip and fell backwards, end over end, hitting the hard wood floor of my library with a resounding whack. I lay upon the floor face up and conscious but unable to move, my eyes locked upon the stub of the hand with it's long bony fingers still wrapped around my throat. I could not move. I must have been paralyzed from the fall. I was alive, but I could not move, but the hand could move and did. It was still seeking to choke the very life out of me.

Then I saw Saunders approach out of the corner of my eye. Now I knew he would help me and pry this hellish thing from my throat.

But would he be in time?

"Mr. Jameson, are you alive? Are you conscious?" he looked down at me frantic with terror and fear, staring at the hand upon my throat with dire dread. I feared he would run off. I know I would have done so, had our situations been reversed. Instead he told me, "You were trying to trap it, now it has trapped you. Your anger brought it to life and once you began to hurt it — I knew it would hurt you. I am sorry."

"Help me!" I pleaded, though no sound could escape my mouth as my lips formed the silent words.

Then I saw Saunders run off, and I suddenly felt deserted and doomed, for I knew I could hold out for only a few moments before I took my last gasp of air and expired.

However, Saunders quickly returned and he held the wooden box from my desktop and placed it close to my head. He opened the lid. Then he withdrew a large pair of snipers put to the demon hand at my throat. He quickly snipped off the thumb of the hand, and as that appendage fell away to the floor in twitching anger, he pulled the rest of the hand from my throat. I thankfully took my first full breath of blessed air as I watched Saunders place the twitching hand and severed thumb into the box. He quickly closed the lid and locked the clasp. Then he picked up the box and left.

The doctors tell me the fall left me paralyzed and that I will never get out of this wheelchair. My life and my writing career are effectively over. Saunders takes care of me now, I am an invalid and quite helpless, thankful for his company. Saunders assures me that he destroyed the thing but the manner of how he did it, he will not discuss with me. When I try to write it is quite impossible. Arthritis coupled with the damage done from the fall make it difficult for me to even hold a pen in my hand. But I try. I try because once that had been my profession, my livelihood. I had been a writer. Now I am a former writer who can not even sign his own name.

I've not been the same since my encounter with the hand. I know Saunders told me he destroyed it but I still realize its presence. I can sometimes feel it's bony fingers pressing upon my throat, but there's something more, something there that is deeper inside of me. Dark thoughts haunt me; it is almost as if something has passed between us. In the middle of the night, when Saunders is sleeping and I am alone praying for dreams of sweet slumber that refuse to come, I know that strange things happen. In the darkness of night my right hand silently picks up a pen and puts it to paper. It writes such terrible things as send my blood to ice. They are demon haunted messages, black realms of malevolence that make me shudder, through I am paralyzed — such is their power.

I have kept these messages hidden from Saunders, but of

course he found the written sheets this morning in my bed and read them in utter terror, but not disbelief. At that moment he realized what I already knew, that the thing had some kind of hold upon me, and it is only then that we looked upon my offending right hand and realized what must be done.

In honor of W. F. Harvey

A Most Extraordinary Man

Scott Edelman

Mrs. Sappleton hadn't thought of that odd Mr. Nuttel since the day he'd fled gibbering from her parlor, due to — or so her niece Vera had said — "a horror of dogs." But as she held a letter addressed from the man's sister in the States, the one who had taken such pleasant meals with her and Vera four years before, it all came flooding back.

"A most extraordinary man," she whispered while studying the envelope, a muttering which caused her niece to ask of whom she spoke. Nothing much escaped the girl's attention, Mrs. Sappleton long ago noticed, often in such a way as to be disturbing.

"Mr. Framton Nuttel," said Mrs. Sappleton. "You remember, that young man who — "

"Oh, I remember *him*, Auntie," said Vera, smiling in a way which Mrs. Sappleton thought, if looked at from the right angle, could almost have been taken for a smirk.

"If you remember him so, then he managed to make a far greater impression on you than he did on me," said Mrs. Sappleton.

"Oh, we shared many things before you came downstairs to join us. Many things."

"And from what you told me, they were not at all things an impressionable girl your age should have heard. Mad dogs on the banks of the Ganges. Sleeping in graves. The young man should have known better."

"But he was sick, Auntie. We should endeavor to forgive him."

"It is good of you to think so, to be able to find in yourself that mercy," said Mrs. Sappleton, and as she held the envelope up to the sunlight which streamed in through the large, open French window, her curiosity changed the subject. "It seems his sister has written me for the first time since that letter of introduction her brother had carried. I wonder why. What could it possibly be about?"

"Oh, read it, Auntie, do!" said Vera, clapping her hands. Mrs. Sappleton was pleased to see the girl, who had only just turned sixteen, show some enthusiasm again. She hadn't seemed quite herself in recent months, had not, in fact, been the girl Mrs. Sappleton helped raise since Mr. Nuttel's brief, eccentric visit, a passing strange coincidence.

Mrs. Sappleton retrieved a letter opener from a low bureau in one corner of the room, slit the envelope lengthwise, cleared her throat, and began to read.

"My dear Mrs. Sappleton," she began. "I wish I were writing you this morning under better circumstances."

Something about the young woman's phrasing made Mrs.

Sappleton pause. As she scanned ahead down the page, a sudden shock coursed through her and weakened her knees. She sat down suddenly, her hand went limp, and the letter fluttered to the rug. Sensing her mistress' distress, Bertie, her husband's little brown spaniel, padded over and licked with concern at the tips of her fingers.

"What wrong?" asked Vera, in a tone suffused with equal parts excitement and worry, though it would have required extensive study to discern which was which.

Mrs. Sappleton waved the hand not being snuffled by the spaniel in vague circles before her, as if searching there for the words she could possibly say that would make the subject matter suitable for Vera's ears. Finding none, she dropped that hand in her lap and spoke in a whisper.

"I don't know that I can ... " she began weakly, then fell to silence.

"Then let me, Auntie!"

Before Mrs. Sappleton could object, Vera had scooped up the letter, and holding it tightly, stood bolt upright before her. Her eyes were bright, as if she were bursting with pride while preparing to recite a poem in school. She cleared her throat, and began to read the unexpected correspondence with an impeccable pronunciation.

"I wish I were writing under better circumstances," she said, strangely channeling the intonations of Miss Nuttel's speech, even though Vera had been but eleven when the two had last spoken. "I have the unfortunate duty of informing you that my beloved brother, whose time on this Earth was so tortured, and whose path through this world was so rocky, has died. I had hoped that the time he spent with you, which as I have so often expressed had been so refreshing for me, might prove equally so for him, might calm his fretful soul, but it was not to be so. He found no cure there. Framton returned from his stay with you as agitated as when he'd departed from my side. He was jittery as ever, starting at the slightest sound, his eyes always darting, his head constantly swiveling atop his shoulders as if he was fearful of something none of the rest of us could see. Eventually, the exhaustion of dealing with his jangled nerves became too much for him, and he ... I will be blunt with you, Mrs. Sappleton. He chose to depart this life.

"I do not blame you, because I remember you and your niece with kindness, and am sure that you each did your best, with your hospitality and your charm, to part the dark clouds which hovered unceasingly over him. Alas, his ailment proved too great to be lifted by any human power. I hope he is now abiding with the One who in His Grace and Mercy may bring all peace to those who would but ask it of Him.

"I hope that if Fate allows I may return to see you and your niece once more someday. Vera was a very interesting young girl, and I am sure that by now she has blossomed into a very interesting young woman. You are both often in my thoughts. Please keep Framton in yours.

"Yours most sincerely, Miss Edith Nuttel"

Vera stopped speaking, but her eyes did not lift from the page. Keeping her head down, her lips moved as she reread a section of the letter.

"Auntie, what did Miss Edith mean when she wrote that, 'he chose to depart this life'? What exactly happened to Mr. Nuttel?"

Mrs. Sappleton looked wearily at her niece, whose eyes

glistened as if she knew more of the answer than her question would have you believe.

"I'm tired, Vera," she said, letting her head drop back against the Morris chair. "Let us talk about this together later."

"Yes, Auntie," said Vera. She folded the letter carefully and slipped it into a pocket. Smiling, she left the drawing room and headed to her bedroom, where she read the letter over and over until it grew far too dark to continue reading, at which point she sat motionless in that darkness and recited it from memory.

The following morning, Mr. Sappleton stepped from the lawn in through the parlor's large open French window and called out to his wife, "Dearie, have you seen Bertie? I can't find him anywhere." He held his shotgun in the crook of one elbow, and his white mackintosh, as yet unmuddied by the day's hunt, was draped over the other.

"That's not like him," said Mrs. Sappleton. "He's usually nipping at your heels by now, begging to be taken along."

"He's not the only one who hasn't been behaving like himself lately," Mr. Sappleton said grumpily.

"Hush, John, she'll hear you."

"And what if she does? A bit of frank talk would do the girl some good. She's been behaving strangely lately. You know that as well as I."

"Oh, I'm sure she'll grow out of it, John. All girls eventually do."

"All girls eventually do what, Auntie?" asked Vera, coming silently into the room.

"How about you?" said Mr. Sappleton roughly to his niece. "Have you seen Bertie?"

Vera placed a forefinger to one pale cheek and tapped it there until her eyes lit up.

"Not since this morning," she said. "I heard him scratching at the door to be let out. He'd spotted a bird he hoped would make him a good breakfast, and I let him have his way. Now what was this about girls?"

Mr. Sappleton harrumphed and stepped over to the open window, where he stared off toward the moor, and the snipe which he hoped waited for him beyond.

"I'm heading off to hunt with those brothers of yours," he said to his wife, "though it doesn't seem right somehow without Bertie. I'll see you later, dearie."

He then dipped his chin toward his niece.

"You, too, Vera."

And then he was gone.

"Will you tell me about girls now, Auntie?" Vera asked as soon as they were alone.

"In a moment," said Mrs. Sappleton, sighing. "But before I do, would you please put this out at the postbox?"

She reached into the folds of her skirt and pulled out an envelope.

"I didn't sleep well last night, and so I wrote a letter of condolence to poor Miss Nuttel. I can't imagine what it would be like to have one's brother ... "

Mrs. Sappleton's voice trailed off, not wishing to expose her niece to such kinds of thoughts.

"Have one's brother what?" asked Vera.

"Never you mind right now," said Mrs. Sappleton firmly. "Just put the letter out front, and then we'll have some tea and talk. Now that you're sixteen, and you're not a girl anymore, we can talk woman to woman. It's long past time for that."

"Yes, Auntie," said Vera, curtsying. She then turned and skipped away toward the front door, like the innocent girl her aunt had first taken in.

Mrs. Sappleton moved to the open window through which she hoped to see one final glimpse of her husband's back, but he had already vanished into the distance. She hoped he would be returning soon. It was early, but something already did not seem right about this day.

Her reverie was interrupted by a high-pitched scream.

Mrs. Sappleton hurried toward the sound, and found her niece at the open front door, staring down at the welcome mat on which was curled the bleeding body of Bertie, quite dead. The letter opener which she had so recently used was plunged into its poor chest, and his eyes stared at them accusingly, as if there'd been something they could have done, but had chosen not to. Mrs. Sappleton grabbed Vera and pulled her to her bosom.

"Stop looking, Vera," she said sternly. "Woman now or not, you shouldn't have to see this."

But even as Mrs. Sappleton pressed her niece against her bosom, Vera twisted her head ever so slightly so that she could peek at the remains of the little brown spaniel, its body twisted, its fur matted with blood. Her expression, unseen by her aunt, was one of both horror and glee.

Mrs. Sappleton sat by the open window, praying for her husband and two younger brothers to arrive home from the marshes soon. But she knew, even as she was engaged in the practice of supplication, that they of course had no idea they had any need to hurry. As far as they believed, it was a day like any other, save for the fact that Bertie was off hunting on his own just as they were, another male, though a four-legged one, doing a male's business, and therefore there was no need for alarm. For the trio of hunters, the day was no different, except for the absence of a dog. While for Mrs. Sappleton, the day was no different, save for the horrid presence of one.

"This is all the fault of a ghost," said Vera, startling her aunt. She'd entered the room so quietly that Mrs. Sappleton had thought herself still alone with her reverie.

"Whose ghost?" Mrs. Sappleton asked reflexively, but realizing the nature of what they were speaking, she quickly changed direction. "There is no such thing as ghosts."

"But, oh, Auntie, there is!" said Vera, wringing her hands before her. "And now that Mr. Nuttel is deceased, his ghost must be mad, just as he was — "

"Vera! There is no need to be insulting! Especially not to the dead."

" — and his spirit has travelled here, and has taken revenge on poor Bertie. Remember, he — "

Vera hesitated a moment before continuing, as if struggling to keep straight the facts of a tale told long ago.

" — he had a horror of dogs."

"I remember no such thing," said Mrs. Sappleton. "I only

remember that you told me so."

"Maybe now that Bertie has passed," said Vera, "poor Mr. Nuttel's soul can rest in peace."

"And maybe you can stop telling such fanciful tales," Mrs. Sappleton said sternly. "Whatever has come over you these recent months? I hardly know when you are telling the truth and when you are … "

Here Mrs. Sappleton stammered, because she had been raised properly by her own aunt, and did not like to make such an accusation as she was about to utter.

" … when you are not."

"Oh, Auntie, I have always tried to tell you the truth. It's just that I can't help myself sometimes. I am a believer in romance at short notice."

"Well, I believe we've had enough of such storytelling and speculation. Let us stick to rational, concrete facts, shall we? No more fabulations."

"If you insist," said Vera, her hand moving to the cloth of her blouse and feeling Mr. Nuttel's letter through the fabric there.

"What's that you have, Vera?"

"Nothing, Auntie," she said, turning quickly away.

"Whatever you've hidden, you must give it to me at once. As I've told you, there will be no secrets in this home."

Mrs. Sappleton stood and approached Vera with one hand outstretched, but before she could compel her niece to produce what had been hidden, her brothers bounded through the open window and into the room.

"Hullo, sister," said Edward, the older of her brothers. He surveyed the room with a smile which turned into a puzzled frown when he did not behold that which he sought.

"Has Bertie returned?" asked Ronnie, her younger. "If not, your husband must be disconsolate without him. You should have seen how he was moping without him on our hunt. I can only imagine how lonely he must be now if his spaniel has not yet turned up."

"Imagine?" asked Mrs. Sappleton anxiously. "Why must we imagine? Where is my husband?"

"You mean he has not yet returned?" asked Edward. "He should have beaten us here by quite a large margin. He left us more than an hour ago."

"Yes," said Ronnie. "Hunting just wasn't the same without Bertie, he said, and so he abandoned us to return for a look. We expected to find them here, frolicking together. Where could they both be?"

Before anyone could answer, Vera leapt up, pointing with a shaking hand toward the open window.

"Lock it!" she shouted. "This is all Mr. Nuttel's fault! He's coming for me just as he came for Bertie!"

"Bertie?" said Ronnie. "What happened to Bertie?"

"Who's Mr. Nuttel?" said Edward. "And why would he be coming for you?"

"I certainly won't be locking any doors," said Mrs. Sappleton. "How else will your uncle be able to get in upon his return? Whatever has come over you?"

"I don't care," said Vera, beginning to cry. "I don't care about any of that. Lock it, lock it you must. I've done something, Auntie. I've done something horrible, and now a haunting has befallen us all."

Her aunt and uncles tried to get her to tell what she had

done, but they could pry nothing from her save tears. As she was inconsolable, Mrs. Sappleton slipped her a jigger of rum and led her up to her bedroom. Edward called out from behind the two women as they fled the parlor.

"I still don't understand," he said. "Who's Mr. Nuttel?"

Somewhere, a dog barked, and it woke Vera to the darkness of her room. She felt somewhat dizzy — whether it was from the alcohol or the excitement of recent events she could not say — and for a moment she wondered if all that she recalled having passed during the preceding day had been but a dream. Hearing that bark of Bertie's surely meant it was so, because how could he bark if he was ...

But then the dog barked yet again, and she shrugged off all symptoms of sleep as easily as she tossed aside her covers. She sat up, heart beating wildly. It surely sounded like Bertie, but ... Bertie could not be alive. She remembered it all now, and there was no doubt as to what had occurred. She had seen him dead. Murdered.

After what Mr. Nuttel had done to Bertie, was she now being haunted by Bertie's ghost as well? Was the spirit of the poor creature bringing this upon their heads as the consequence of all her fabrications?

She tiptoed to the window, hoping that in the slowly increasing moonlight she could spot whatever beast it was that had made the sound. Perhaps (she told herself, even though she doubted it could be so) she had only mistaken an owl for a spaniel. But as she stared out her window and down across the lawn, no further barking came, and so she had no idea in which direction to look in hopes of locating it.

Then she saw something — a white glow that grew more prominent as the moon rose in the sky. Her heart jumped in her chest. Was this Mr. Nuttel's ghost, come to punish her? She stared, willing herself not to blink, waiting for the shimmering blotch to move, as surely it must ... but it did not. Then she realized — it was nothing more than her uncle's white mackintosh, reflecting the moonlight. Had he left it hanging on a tree in the yard upon his return? But if so, why had none of them noticed it before?

She slid open the window and scuttled down the trellis, ignoring the occasional scratch of a thorn. She would retrieve the mackintosh and bring it back to Auntie and Uncle, who had to be home by now, home and asleep the next room over, and things would again be as they had been. But once she dropped to the ground and began walking toward the glow, she saw by the shifting of its outline that — it wasn't just the coat, it was her uncle himself, leaning motionless against the tree, head tilted back against the bark, studying the night sky as she approached.

"Uncle, what are you doing out here?" asked Vera. "You have worried poor Auntie so much!"

He did not answer her. She drew nearer and touched his hand so he would look down and notice her. Could he have fallen asleep out here in the cool air? But ... no. Now that she was before him, she could see ... his hair was matted with blood, mirroring Bertie's fur. But no knife had made his wounds.

He had been struck by a rock.

She tugged at his hand, and his head fell forward, his chin against his chest. His eyes, though wide, saw her not.

She shrieked, pulling back her hand, and as she did so, her Uncle toppled forward, knocking her off her feet, pinning her beneath him to the lawn. She could not move, could barely breath from the sheer weight of him, and soon lost consciousness beneath the stars.

When Vera woke, Auntie was peering down at her, a stern expression on her face.

"What are you doing out here in the cold and damp, Vera?" she asked. "This is no place for a young girl to sleep."

"But Uncle — "

"What about Uncle? He still has yet to return."

Vera groggily propped herself up on her elbows. There was no white mackintosh. No Uncle. And she looked down the length of her nightshirt, as far as she could tell, there was no blood either.

"I saw him," insisted Vera. "He was here. He had been hurt, and he was — "

"I thought we agreed there would be no more fanciful tales. And especially none so hurtful to me as that."

"But I'm not lying, I — "

"Enough!" barked Mrs. Sappleton, louder than Vera had ever remembered her.

Mrs. Sappleton yanked her niece to her feet and pulled

her roughly toward the house.

"Let's get you back to your room," she said.

"But I don't want to go there," said Vera as she was pulled in through the open window and up the stairs. She looked back at it in horror and grew hysterical. It had all begun with an open window, a window which her aunt now refused to lock.

"I don't want to be alone," she howled. "Please, Auntie, don't leave me alone tonight. You mustn't. You can't!"

Mrs. Sappleton pushed Vera into her bed, but as she arranged the covers and looked down at her trembling niece, her heart softened.

"Move over slightly, child," she said. "Allow me to get in bed beside you, and we'll sleep as we first did when you came to live with Uncle and me. All will be better in the morning. You'll see. Things are always better in the morning."

Were they? Vera had no way of knowing, but as she snuggled closer against her Auntie, she found comfort there, and fell quickly asleep. She did not dream, and if there was further barking in the night, she either did not hear it or slept so deeply that it did not wake her.

When Vera woke to the bright sunshine streaming into her room through the window she had opened and climbed through the night before, she felt a clammy dampness about her, and her first thought was, "Not again."

To wet yourself at her age, especially after being told you

were a woman, was embarrassing enough, but to do so while your Auntie was sleeping beside you was positively unbearable. Vera disentangled herself from her Auntie and as she pulled away she realized ... the wetness was not her own.

She tilted her head back toward Auntie's face ever so slowly, somehow knowing what she would find there, and saw her wrinkled cheeks covered in blood. The blanket which had been pulled to her neck was soaked as well. Vera leapt back, rolling off the bed and onto the Oriental rug, unintentionally pulling the soiled blanket with her, which made her shriek even more, and she slapped at it, coiling herself in it more and more the harder she fought to free herself, until she finally broke away and could toss the sodden blanket aside.

And there, now that she could see again, was Framton Nuttel, sitting on the sill of the open window, wearing her uncle's white mackintosh, the front of which was drenched with blood.

"Hello, Vera," he said. It was only when he spoke that she noticed his hands were scarlet, too.

"You're ... alive? But I thought — "

"You thought so many things. Too many things. Like your story about the tragedy that befell your dead uncles and the eccentricity of your pining aunt. My nervous condition had me on the edge, Vera. And your fancies pushed me over that edge."

"But your sister's letter? She said — "

"My sister said nothing. My sister — thanks to you, thanks to what you forced me to become — is no longer capable of anything. *I* wrote that letter. And then I returned. Returned to tell you that you are a bad little girl. And to make you pay.

And to make all who loved you and all whom you loved pay."

He made a move to rise, but Vera held a hand toward him and he paused.

"Stay where you are," she said. "I have but to make a sound, and my uncles will be in here immediately. Then they will thrash you for what you have done."

Mr. Nuttel smiled, but now there was a flicker there that remained from the nervous uncertainty of old.

"Your uncles are not with us, Vera. They returned to their own homes and spent the night with their own families. You and I are the only living things within earshot."

"They are too here," said Vera, setting her jaw. "They could not bear to leave their sister alone without her husband, and so they remained in the guest room. You know nothing of a brother's love, Mr. Nuttel. All I need to do is scream. And believe me. I will."

He knew there was no one else there, he *knew* it, but yet when the words fell from her lips, she told the lie with such flair, that for a fleeting moment, he believed her, just as he had believed her when she had told him that ridiculous story so many months ago. So when she inhaled as if to scream, he hesitated when he should have leapt upon her, and she instead leapt upon him, pushing him out the open window.

As he tumbled back, she slammed the window shut, locking it quickly, regretting the falsity of her lie, and wishing that her uncles had been there to rescue her. But they of course were not.

She could see Mr. Nuttel rise to his feet and hobble around the house, and suddenly remembered — the open window downstairs through which Auntie had hoped her husband would return, but through which he would never step again — Auntie had left it open, she had *insisted* on leaving it open, why had she not believed her?

She raced downstairs, and into the parlor, and did not find Mr. Nuttel there. She was in time! The fall had made him lame, and had given her the moments she needed. She leapt at the door, began slamming it on its hinges, but before she could seal herself inside, Mr. Nuttel blocked it with a bloody hand. She could hear the bones of his fingers crack as the door hit them, but his face showed no pain. His madness had transported him beyond its reach.

He bruted the door open violently, the force of which knocked her back onto the rug. He stepped through the open window looking so, so tall.

"Mr. Nuttel," she said, voice quivering, seeking in her mind for some tale that would divert him, and finding none. "What is it you are planning to do to me? Am I to suffer the same fate as Bertie and Uncle and Auntie?"

"Oh, no," he said, letting the white mackintosh, now stained with red, fall from his shoulders and revealing that what lay beneath was equally as horrifying and bloodied. "I have something very special planned for you, Vera. Because, you see, romance at short notice is also *my* specialty ... "

In honor of Saki

The Monkey's Paw

W. W. Jacobs

Without, the night was cold and wet, but in the small parlour of Laburnam Villa the blinds were drawn and the fire burned brightly. Father and son were at chess, the former, who possessed ideas about the game involving radical changes, putting his king into such sharp and unnecessary perils that it even provoked comment from the white-haired old lady knitting placidly by the fire.

"Hark at the wind," said Mr. White, who, having seen a fatal mistake after it was too late, was amiably desirous of preventing his son from seeing it.

"I'm listening," said the latter, grimly surveying the board as he stretched out his hand. "Check."

"I should hardly think that he'd come to-night," said his father, with his hand poised over the board.

"Mate," replied the son.

"That's the worst of living so far out," bawled Mr. White, with sudden and unlooked-for violence; "of all the beastly, slushy, out-of-the-way places to live in, this is the worst. Pathway's a bog, and the road's a torrent. I don't know what people are thinking about. I suppose because only two houses in the road are let, they think it doesn't matter."

"Never mind, dear," said his wife, soothingly; "perhaps you'll win the next one."

Mr. White looked up sharply, just in time to intercept a knowing glance between mother and son. The words died away on his lips, and he hid a guilty grin in his thin grey beard.

"There he is," said Herbert White, as the gate banged to loudly and heavy footsteps came toward the door.

The old man rose with hospitable haste, and opening the door, was heard condoling with the new arrival. The new arrival also condoled with himself, so that Mrs. White said, "Tut, tut!" and coughed gently as her husband entered the room, followed by a tall, burly man, beady of eye and rubicund of visage.

"Sergeant-Major Morris," he said, introducing him.

The sergeant-major shook hands, and taking the proffered seat by the fire, watched contentedly while his host got out whiskey and tumblers and stood a small copper kettle on the fire.

At the third glass his eyes got brighter, and he began to talk, the little family circle regarding with eager interest this visitor from distant parts, as he squared his broad shoulders in the chair and spoke of wild scenes and doughty deeds; of wars and plagues and strange peoples.

"Twenty-one years of it," said Mr. White, nodding at his wife and son. "When he went away he was a slip of a youth in the warehouse. Now look at him."

"He don't look to have taken much harm," said Mrs. White, politely.

"I'd like to go to India myself," said the old man, "just to look round a bit, you know."

"Better where you are," said the sergeant-major, shaking his head. He put down the empty glass, and sighing softly, shook it again.

"I should like to see those old temples and fakirs and jugglers," said the old man. "What was that you started telling me the other day about a monkey's paw or something, Morris?"

"Nothing," said the soldier, hastily. "Leastways nothing worth hearing."

"Monkey's paw?" said Mrs. White, curiously.

"Well, it's just a bit of what you might call magic, perhaps," said the sergeant-major, offhandedly.

His three listeners leaned forward eagerly. The visitor absent-mindedly put his empty glass to his lips and then set it down again. His host filled it for him.

"To look at," said the sergeant-major, fumbling in his pocket, "it's just an ordinary little paw, dried to a mummy."

He took something out of his pocket and proffered it. Mrs. White drew back with a grimace, but her son, taking it, examined it curiously.

"And what is there special about it?" inquired Mr. White as he took it from his son, and having examined it, placed it upon the table.

"It had a spell put on it by an old fakir," said the sergeant-major, "a very holy man. He wanted to show that fate ruled people's lives, and that those who interfered with it did so to their sorrow. He put a spell on it so that three separate men could each have three wishes from it."

His manner was so impressive that his hearers were conscious that their light laughter jarred somewhat.

"Well, why don't you have three, sir?" said Herbert White, cleverly.

The soldier regarded him in the way that middle age is wont to regard presumptuous youth. "I have," he said, quietly, and his blotchy face whitened.

"And did you really have the three wishes granted?" asked Mrs. White.

"I did," said the sergeant-major, and his glass tapped against his strong teeth.

"And has anybody else wished?" persisted the old lady.

"The first man had his three wishes. Yes," was the reply; "I don't know what the first two were, but the third was for death. That's how I got the paw."

His tones were so grave that a hush fell upon the group.

"If you've had your three wishes, it's no good to you now, then, Morris," said the old man at last. "What do you keep it for?"

The soldier shook his head. "Fancy, I suppose," he said, slowly. "I did have some idea of selling it, but I don't think I will. It has caused enough mischief already. Besides, people won't buy. They think it's a fairy tale; some of them, and those who do think anything of it want to try it first and pay me afterward."

"If you could have another three wishes," said the old man, eyeing him keenly, "would you have them?"

"I don't know," said the other. "I don't know."

He took the paw, and dangling it between his forefinger and thumb, suddenly threw it upon the fire. White, with a slight cry, stooped down and snatched it off.

"Better let it burn," said the soldier, solemnly.

"If you don't want it, Morris," said the other, "give it to me."

"I won't," said his friend, doggedly. "I threw it on the fire. If you keep it, don't blame me for what happens. Pitch it on the fire again like a sensible man."

The other shook his head and examined his new possession closely. "How do you do it?" he inquired.

"Hold it up in your right hand and wish aloud," said the sergeant-major, "but I warn you of the consequences."

"Sounds like the Arabian Nights," said Mrs. White, as she rose and began to set the supper. "Don't you think you might wish for four pairs of hands for me?"

Her husband drew the talisman from pocket, and then all three burst into laughter as the sergeant-major, with a look of alarm on his face, caught him by the arm.

"If you must wish," he said, gruffly, "wish for something sensible."

Mr. White dropped it back in his pocket, and placing chairs, motioned his friend to the table. In the business of supper the talisman was partly forgotten, and afterward the three sat listening in an enthralled fashion to a second instalment of the soldier's adventures in India.

"If the tale about the monkey's paw is not more truthful than those he has been telling us," said Herbert, as the door closed behind their guest, just in time for him to catch the last train, "we sha'nt make much out of it."

"Did you give him anything for it, father?" inquired Mrs. White, regarding her husband closely.

"A trifle," said he, colouring slightly. "He didn't want it, but I made him take it. And he pressed me again to throw it away."

"Likely," said Herbert, with pretended horror. "Why, we're going to be rich, and famous and happy. Wish to be an emperor, father, to begin with; then you can't be henpecked."

He darted round the table, pursued by the maligned Mrs. White armed with an antimacassar.

Mr. White took the paw from his pocket and eyed it dubiously. "I don't know what to wish for, and that's a fact," he said, slowly. "It seems to me I've got all I want."

"If you only cleared the house, you'd be quite happy, wouldn't you?" said Herbert, with his hand on his shoulder. "Well, wish for two hundred pounds, then; that 'll just do it."

His father, smiling shamefacedly at his own credulity, held up the talisman, as his son, with a solemn face, somewhat marred by a wink at his mother, sat down at the piano and struck a few impressive chords.

"I wish for two hundred pounds," said the old man distinctly.

A fine crash from the piano greeted the words, interrupted by a shuddering cry from the old man. His wife and son ran toward him.

"It moved," he cried, with a glance of disgust at the object as it lay on the floor.

"As I wished, it twisted in my hand like a snake."

"Well, I don't see the money," said his son as he picked it

up and placed it on the table, "and I bet I never shall."

"It must have been your fancy, father," said his wife, regarding him anxiously.

He shook his head. "Never mind, though; there's no harm done, but it gave me a shock all the same."

They sat down by the fire again while the two men finished their pipes. Outside, the wind was higher than ever, and the old man started nervously at the sound of a door banging upstairs. A silence unusual and depressing settled upon all three, which lasted until the old couple rose to retire for the night.

"I expect you'll find the cash tied up in a big bag in the middle of your bed," said Herbert, as he bade them good-night, "and something horrible squatting up on top of the wardrobe watching you as you pocket your ill-gotten gains."

He sat alone in the darkness, gazing at the dying fire, and seeing faces in it. The last face was so horrible and so simian that he gazed at it in amazement. It got so vivid that, with a little uneasy laugh, he felt on the table for a glass containing a little water to throw over it. His hand grasped the monkey's paw, and with a little shiver he wiped his hand on his coat and went up to bed.

In the brightness of the wintry sun next morning as it streamed over the breakfast table he laughed at his fears. There was an air of prosaic wholesomeness about the room which it had lacked on the previous night, and the dirty, shrivelled little paw was pitched on the sideboard with a carelessness which betokened no great belief in its virtues.

"I suppose all old soldiers are the same," said Mrs. White. "The idea of our listening to such nonsense! How could wishes be granted in these days? And if they could, how could two hundred pounds hurt you, father?"

"Might drop on his head from the sky," said the frivolous Herbert.

"Morris said the things happened so naturally," said his father, "that you might if you so wished attribute it to coincidence."

"Well, don't break into the money before I come back," said Herbert as he rose from the table. "I'm afraid it'll turn you into a mean, avaricious man, and we shall have to disown you."

His mother laughed, and following him to the door, watched him down the road; and returning to the breakfast table, was very happy at the expense of her husband's credulity. All of which did not prevent her from scurrying to the door at the postman's knock, nor prevent her from referring somewhat shortly to retired sergeant-majors of bibulous habits when she found that the post brought a tailor's bill.

"Herbert will have some more of his funny remarks, I expect, when he comes home," she said, as they sat at dinner.

"I dare say," said Mr. White, pouring himself out some beer; "but for all that, the thing moved in my hand; that I'll swear to."

"You thought it did," said the old lady soothingly.

"I say it did," replied the other. "There was no thought about it; I had just—- What's the matter?"

His wife made no reply. She was watching the mysterious

movements of a man outside, who, peering in an undecided fashion at the house, appeared to be trying to make up his mind to enter. In mental connection with the two hundred pounds, she noticed that the stranger was well dressed, and wore a silk hat of glossy newness. Three times he paused at the gate, and then walked on again. The fourth time he stood with his hand upon it, and then with sudden resolution flung it open and walked up the path. Mrs. White at the same moment placed her hands behind her, and hurriedly unfastening the strings of her apron, put that useful article of apparel beneath the cushion of her chair.

She brought the stranger, who seemed ill at ease, into the room. He gazed at her furtively, and listened in a preoccupied fashion as the old lady apologized for the appearance of the room, and her husband's coat, a garment which he usually reserved for the garden. She then waited as patiently as her sex would permit, for him to broach his business, but he was at first strangely silent.

"I—was asked to call," he said at last, and stooped and picked a piece of cotton from his trousers. "I come from 'Maw and Meggins.'"

The old lady started. "Is anything the matter?" she asked, breathlessly. "Has anything happened to Herbert? What is it? What is it?"

Her husband interposed. "There, there, mother," he said, hastily. "Sit down, and don't jump to conclusions. You've not brought bad news, I'm sure, sir;" and he eyed the other wistfully.

"I'm sorry—" began the visitor.

"Is he hurt?" demanded the mother, wildly.

The visitor bowed in assent. "Badly hurt," he said, quietly, "but he is not in any pain."

"Oh, thank God!" said the old woman, clasping her hands. "Thank God for that! Thank—"

She broke off suddenly as the sinister meaning of the assurance dawned upon her and she saw the awful confirmation of her fears in the other's averted face. She caught her breath, and turning to her slower-witted husband, laid her trembling old hand upon his. There was a long silence.

"He was caught in the machinery," said the visitor at length in a low voice.

"Caught in the machinery," repeated Mr. White, in a dazed fashion, "yes."

He sat staring blankly out at the window, and taking his wife's hand between his own, pressed it as he had been wont to do in their old courting-days nearly forty years before.

"He was the only one left to us," he said, turning gently to the visitor. "It is hard."

The other coughed, and rising, walked slowly to the window. "The firm wished me to convey their sincere sympathy with you in your great loss," he said, without looking round. "I beg that you will understand I am only their servant and merely obeying orders."

There was no reply; the old woman's face was white, her eyes staring, and her breath inaudible; on the husband's face was a look such as his friend the sergeant might have carried into his first action.

"I was to say that 'Maw and Meggins' disclaim all responsibility," continued the other. "They admit no liability at all, but in consideration of your son's services, they wish to present you with a certain sum as compensation."

Mr. White dropped his wife's hand, and rising to his feet, gazed with a look of horror at his visitor. His dry lips shaped the words, "How much?"

"Two hundred pounds," was the answer.

Unconscious of his wife's shriek, the old man smiled faintly, put out his hands like a sightless man, and dropped, a senseless heap, to the floor.

In the huge new cemetery, some two miles distant, the old people buried their dead, and came back to a house steeped in shadow and silence. It was all over so quickly that at first they could hardly realize it, and remained in a state of expectation as though of something else to happen — something else which was to lighten this load, too heavy for old hearts to bear.

But the days passed, and expectation gave place to resignation—the hopeless resignation of the old, sometimes miscalled, apathy. Sometimes they hardly exchanged a word, for now they had nothing to talk about, and their days were long to weariness.

It was about a week after that the old man, waking suddenly in the night, stretched out his hand and found himself alone. The room was in darkness, and the sound of subdued weeping came from the window. He raised himself in bed and listened.

"Come back," he said, tenderly. "You will be cold."

"It is colder for my son," said the old woman, and wept afresh.

The sound of her sobs died away on his ears. The bed was warm, and his eyes heavy with sleep. He dozed fitfully, and then slept until a sudden wild cry from his wife awoke him with a start.

"The paw!" she cried wildly. "The monkey's paw!"

He started up in alarm. "Where? Where is it? What's the matter?"

She came stumbling across the room toward him. "I want it," she said, quietly. "You've not destroyed it?"

"It's in the parlour, on the bracket," he replied, marvelling. "Why?"

She cried and laughed together, and bending over, kissed his cheek.

"I only just thought of it," she said, hysterically. "Why didn't I think of it before? Why didn't you think of it?"

"Think of what?" he questioned.

"The other two wishes," she replied, rapidly. "We've only had one."

"Was not that enough?" he demanded, fiercely.

"No," she cried, triumphantly; "we'll have one more. Go down and get it quickly, and wish our boy alive again."

The man sat up in bed and flung the bedclothes from his quaking limbs. "Good God, you are mad!" he cried, aghast.

"Get it," she panted; "get it quickly, and wish—Oh, my boy, my boy!"

Her husband struck a match and lit the candle. "Get back to bed," he said, unsteadily. "You don't know what you are saying."

"We had the first wish granted," said the old woman, feverishly; "why not the second?"

"A coincidence," stammered the old man.

"Go and get it and wish," cried his wife, quivering with excitement.

The old man turned and regarded her, and his voice shook. "He has been dead ten days, and besides he—I would not tell you else, but—I could only recognize him by his clothing. If he was too terrible for you to see then, how now?"

"Bring him back," cried the old woman, and dragged him toward the door. "Do you think I fear the child I have nursed?"

He went down in the darkness, and felt his way to the parlour, and then to the mantelpiece. The talisman was in its place, and a horrible fear that the unspoken wish might bring his mutilated son before him ere he could escape from the room seized upon him, and he caught his breath as he found that he had lost the direction of the door. His brow cold with sweat, he felt his way round the table, and groped along the wall until he found himself in the small passage with the unwholesome thing in his hand.

Even his wife's face seemed changed as he entered the room. It was white and expectant, and to his fears seemed to have an unnatural look upon it. He was afraid of her.

"Wish!" she cried, in a strong voice.

"It is foolish and wicked," he faltered.

"Wish!" repeated his wife.

He raised his hand. "I wish my son alive again."

The talisman fell to the floor, and he regarded it fearfully. Then he sank trembling into a chair as the old woman, with burning eyes, walked to the window and raised the blind.

He sat until he was chilled with the cold, glancing occasionally at the figure of the old woman peering through the window. The candle-end, which had burned below the rim of the china candlestick, was throwing pulsating shadows on the ceiling and walls, until, with a flicker larger than the rest, it expired. The old man, with an unspeakable sense of relief at the failure of the talisman, crept back to his bed, and a minute or two afterward the old woman came silently and apathetically beside him.

Neither spoke, but lay silently listening to the ticking of the clock. A stair creaked, and a squeaky mouse scurried noisily through the wall. The darkness was oppressive, and after lying for some time screwing up his courage, he took the box of matches, and striking one, went downstairs for a candle.

At the foot of the stairs the match went out, and he paused to strike another; and at the same moment a knock, so quiet and stealthy as to be scarcely audible, sounded on the front door.

The matches fell from his hand and spilled in the passage. He stood motionless, his breath suspended until the knock was repeated. Then he turned and fled swiftly back to his room, and closed the door behind him. A third knock sounded through the house.

"What's that?" cried the old woman, starting up.

"A rat," said the old man in shaking tones—"a rat. It passed me on the stairs."

His wife sat up in bed listening. A loud knock resounded through the house.

"It's Herbert!" she screamed. "It's Herbert!"

She ran to the door, but her husband was before her, and catching her by the arm, held her tightly.

"What are you going to do?" he whispered hoarsely.

"It's my boy; it's Herbert!" she cried, struggling mechanically. "I forgot it was two miles away. What are you holding me for? Let go. I must open the door."

"For God's sake don't let it in," cried the old man, trembling.

"You're afraid of your own son," she cried, struggling. "Let me go. I'm coming, Herbert; I'm coming."

There was another knock, and another. The old woman with a sudden wrench broke free and ran from the room. Her husband followed to the landing, and called after her appealingly as she hurried downstairs. He heard the chain rattle back and the bottom bolt drawn slowly and stiffly from the socket. Then the old woman's voice, strained and panting.

"The bolt," she cried, loudly. "Come down. I can't reach it."

But her husband was on his hands and knees groping wildly on the floor in search of the paw. If he could only find it before the thing outside got in. A perfect fusillade of knocks reverberated through the house, and he heard the scraping of a chair as his wife put it down in the passage against the door. He heard the creaking of the bolt as it came slowly back, and at the same moment he found the monkey's paw, and frantically breathed his third and last wish.

The knocking ceased suddenly, although the echoes of it were still in the house. He heard the chair drawn back, and the door opened. A cold wind rushed up the staircase, and a long loud wail of disappointment and misery from his wife gave him courage to run down to her side, and then to the gate beyond. The street lamp flickering opposite shone on a quiet and deserted road.

The Monkey's Other Paw

Alegría Luna Luz

"If you make a wish be careful, be sure the devil is not listening."

– Anonymous

In the town the children called her "The Monkey Mother." She wandered the town's gas-lit streets and the women would always cross themselves after she passed. They heard she had summoned her son from the grave and had lost her mind and most likely her soul on account of her selfish act of resurrection. They thought she, in her envy, could deprive them of their sons just back from the battlefields. The only women not afraid to talk to The Mother were women with loved ones that had not returned from the war. Many women full with woe wandering the town. They would stop her in the street to ask about the monkey's paw. When accosted, The Mother always put her hands to her white hair and ran away to the Laburnum Villa on the ridge outside the town where she lived. The most persistent pursuer was Nanni, whose daughter Antoinette had drowned last fall. Some in town said it was a suicide.

Late one afternoon Nanni saw The Mother walking in the street and ran up to her and said, "I want my daughter back, even if only for a minute." The Mother looked ill but for once did not run off. Her mad eyes peered at Nanni. "Leave me alone, for mercy's sake. It would be better for you if you keep your daughter's face within your memory or, if you believe in the hereafter, wait to see her in the Kingdom to come."

The only memory in Nanni's mind was the open casket with her only child in it. Perhaps only The Mother could imagine what it meant to be deprived of her child forever and yet have hope for a reunion in this world, however brief. Nanni felt like screaming and this must have been apparent because The Mother turned and hurried away.

"I don't want to live without her," Nanni called after her.

"I can do nothing for you; she's gone forever."

"You don't believe that." With angry, pitiful eyes, the bereaved woman followed The Mother. "Antonette was in love with your son. Your son could have been my son-in-law."

The Mother stopped and turned. "You wicked person!" All the blood had gone to her head.

Nanni, perhaps sensing that the anguish within her could

never be expressed by words, still tried to put across her feelings.

"You know the truth of my words. Your son may have kept his love a secret to you but you must have sensed it. Mothers know these things. I tell you they were sweethearts."

The Mother's son did not tell her everything. In truth she had been thinking about this for a long time. Her son had always been a quiet, shy boy. She remembered he had changed a great deal after he started working at the warehouse, before the accident. She thought of him as her child but he was also a young man. That was a little over a year ago, when he was nineteen. She knew that he had started smoking cigarettes and even drinking. She could smell these vices on him when he came home late at night on the weekend and saw the marks on his neck just below his shirt collar.

The Mother glared at Nanni and remembered the night of the visit from the retired Sergeant Major. "What do you know of the monkey's paw?" The Mother asked.

Nanni repeated the story told around the village.

How the Sergeant Major, home from service in India, had brought the thing into their house. He told them that an old Fakir, a holy man, had a spell put on it. The Fakir wanted to show that fate ruled people's lives, and that those who interfered with it did so to their grief. He selected the paw as a talisman and put a spell on it so that three separate men could each have three wishes from it. That night, knowing the evil in the thing, the Sergeant Major threw the paw into the fireplace where her husband pulled it out of the flames.

Later, after the Sergeant Major had gone, her husband wished for 200 pounds and the monkey's paw had twitched in his hand. The next day they received news of the accidental death of their son Herbert on the job, caught in the machinery, and a cash compensation for that exact sum the husband had wished for the night before.

It was all a coincidence said the husband, but not quite a fortnight after the accident The Mother had induced her husband to use the paw to wish their boy alive again, to call him back from his grave. It was only when a loud knock resounded through the house did the father lose his nerve and used the third and last wish to breathe the mutilated thing outside the door away before his wife could let it in.

"My husband was never the same afterwards. He seemed to wither away, like the mummified talisman that had brought all our misery. I believe he felt guilt at making the first wish and wishing his own son away."

The one thing Nanni did not know was that on the night, eight months after the passing of their son, The Mother's husband died quietly in bed and before they took his body away, she laid her head down on the pillow next to him and vowed, "I will have another chance to get my family back."

At the husband's wake and funeral The Mother was calm and dignified, and afterwards when everyone had gathered at her house she had told them all the story of the monkey's paw. Some of the attendees at the wake thought her grief had made her mad but a few believed her story, especially when The Mother pulled the monkey's paw from her handbag and held it up for all to see.

The paw looked like one of the gnarled, stunted, tiny trees that grew in the glass window box in the house owned by the Japan-born foreigner, and it chilled all who saw it.

"But you do not know that the monkey's paw has a mate," The Mother said softly enough that Nanni had to lean forward to hear. "After my husband's funeral I also angrily pitched the paw into the fireplace. It did not burn and remained whole within the flame. I soon discovered the reason for this when one day the Sergeant Major returned. He told me he must retrieve the paw and restore it to its original owner. I had hid it. I could see that he was under some compulsion to retrieve the talisman. I would not give it back so easily. I told him I would only trade for another talisman—one with three new wishes. The Sergeant Major was horrified by my request but could not sway me, so he left.

"He returned a month later with the monkey's other paw and the exchange was made, but there was one catch with the new talisman. Just as we women cannot vote, I cannot express the wishes myself. The Fakir put a spell on the original monkey's paw so that men could have three wishes from it and he had done the same with the second paw. The Sergeant Major said the new paw had three wishes and there would be no more after that. I accepted that this was the best he could do. After what happened the first time when my husband lost faith and undid my wish I knew I could not trust a man again. But I cannot make it work on my own."

The Mother paused and looked closely at the woman in the gathering gloom and saw that her face really did show traces of suffering. "My son had no chance, there were no doctors summoned to the accident. All his co-workers assumed him dead. Only my husband was allowed to go into the morgue. The casket was closed. I didn't even get to say goodbye to him the last morning when he left for work."

Nanni spoke. "I have a nephew!" She said excitedly. " His mind has not formed. His father calls him a dullard and per- haps this is true but the boy is capable of accomplishing un- complicated tasks assigned to him and even reciting passages from Shakespeare without any deviation."

A light was lit in The Mother's mind, everything became illuminated: she could see the nephew reciting the wishes; she could see her son and husband standing on the thresh- old of the house and she saw father and son playing checkers together again, and a wish still left for the woman standing before her to retrieve her daughter.

"Everything will depend on the wording of the wishes," The Mother said.

The parlor was exactly the same, and just as before her son's death there was a checkerboard on the table and some drinking glasses. That night had been set for the event. The boy, whose name was Ayden, held his aunt's hand when they appeared at the door and entered The Mother's house. He appeared to be a gentle boy who had the outward appearance of a young man. Nanni had told The Mother that the boy spent more time around adults than boys or girls his own age. Children his own age only bullied him.

"Is this where we are having the play?" the boy asked.

"Yes," Nanni said, "I will give you the words very soon."

"Everybody coming here? Like in school?" The boy appeared exhilarated. "I want to hear the words now."

"In a moment," Nanni said to the boy, then turned to the Mother. "He believes we are performing a scene from a play. He has some talent for remembering lines and can even recite with some control of emotions."

"Is he up to it?"

"Yes," Nanni said.

The Mother prepared the room by yet again rearranging the chairs around the chess set, shifting a photograph of her son on the mantle, and then she left the room. She returned with her handbag and rummaged through it. She took out a small purse that contained the paw wrapped in a handkerchief. In a second she was holding two sheets of note paper in one hand and the monkey's paw in the other. She sat at the table and copied a few lines from one sheet to a second sheet, blotted the ink and handed both sheets to Nanni. Nanni took up the notes and compared them carefully.

"They are exact," she said. "We will bring back your husband and son in one wish."

The Mother looked at her. "Yes, my family, intact as they were the night the first monkey's paw came into this house."

"Then my Antoinette with the second wish – leaving the last wish as a safeguard."

The Mother spoke rapidly, and in an authoritative manner. "Are you ready?"

Nanni nodded and handed The Mother one of the sheets of paper.

She took the boy aside and spoke to him quietly, reading from the paper. She already knew the words, but both mothers had agreed that a cheat sheet would allow for no mistakes

– of course the boy himself could not read. Nanni thought without the paper she would not have the presence of mind to go through with the deed.

Nanni began reciting into the boy's ear and let him repeat the words in her own ear. After a bit they took a break.

Ayden recited to himself, then turned to his aunt. "Everybody not here to watch," he said.

"They are coming soon. Remember you must wait for my cue to speak. Now repeat your lines."

The Mother occupied herself with getting wood into the fireplace.

"I need a drink," Nanni said softly as the boy repeated the words she had read.

"Now, now," The Mother said soothingly. "We'll have a drink when everyone gets here."

"Everybody here," the boy parroted.

Nanni spent more than an hour coaching the boy, teaching him the exact incantations in the proper order. The Mother watched them quietly.

At one point Nanni said, "That is the best I can do. He either has it or he doesn't."

"Don't jinx it!" said the Mother. "No more waiting." She handed the paw to the boy. "Have him hold it up in his right hand and wish aloud."

"Right," said Nanni. "Now Ayden, say your first line."

Innocent of the guile behind the words he spoke, Ayden loudly recited the first wish.

The paw twitched alive in his hand and Ayden dropped it in fright. "It moved!"

The Mother was prepared. "It has a clockwork mechanism

inside." She snatched the paw from the floor and placed it on the table.

A sound from outside penetrated the door. This was not a fancied sound, nor one made by footsteps on the flat-stones of the road. The room was warm from the fireplace. At first Nanni thought she had heard nothing more than the pop and crackling of improperly dried bark bits burning in the chimney. Nanni felt the strength in her legs leaving her and she sat at one of the chairs meant for the men, leaning against the top of the table with one elbow, her mouth open and eyes wide.

The Mother was too restless to sit and paced along the front windows. For one moment a flicker of doubt entered her gray eyes, but this feeling quickly faded. Still, she was too afraid to look out into the darkness. The cemetery lay two miles away. She knew she was in her right mind even if she could not convince anyone else. She also knew that her family would never be separated again.

A loud pounding sounded at the door without any footsteps or voices to give notice. The Mother remembered that they did not have keys in their pockets.

"It is unlocked, you don't have to knock," she called out. The Mother threw open the big door.

Nanni had her eyes closed.

The husband came in first, followed by their son Herbert. Both appeared whole.

Mother called out not his name but the endearing term she had not used since their first year of marriage.

"What is wrong with you?" the father asked.

Nanni opened her eyes at the sound of his voice.

The Mother broke into a smile and embraced first her husband and then her son, who looked at his mother suspiciously.

"Why is the lamp unlit outside? I would have lit a match to see my way if one had been in my pocket. Bring me a drink, I am parched...bring drinks for both of us. If I didn't know the way I would have been lost in the dark and cold. It is pitch black out there. Not even a moon out...."

"I could bring my hand within an inch of my face and still not see it," the son added. "And I couldn't seem to get a decent breath into my lungs."

Mother and son looked at each other for a moment, then Herbert saw Nanni and Ayden in the corner of the room.

"I wanted to surprise you," The Mother said.

The flames in the fireplace leaped and sputtered.

"I'm glad you are both back home," Nanni said more loudly then she meant to. Her uneasy feeling had not faded.

"Glad?" asked her husband, his face sagged as though weights pulled down at his cheeks.

"So glad," The Mother repeated.

Nanni took up the monkey's paw, rose from her seat and went to face Ayden. She handed the paw to him. "Now call for Antoinette."

"Say it." her voice now shrill. "Make the second wish."

The husband glanced at Ayden's hand then turned to his wife. "You still have that bloody paw."

"No dear, this is another one. The one you remember has gone back to that old Faker."

The husband was silent and stared at the monkey's paw in Ayden's right hand with a sudden keen awareness.

"Call Antoinette back!" Nanni yelled at Ayden.

The son looked at his mother. "Is Antonette here?"

"Ahh, ahh," murmured The Mother and she looked away. Ayden was speaking but she could not hear him and she turned to face the boy.

The paw twitched in Ayden's hand. This time Ayden did not drop it.

A woman's faint voice called in the distance. The son ran towards the door.

The voice called again. A horrible expression came across the husband's face. There was a strained moment of silence as the son's body blocked the opened door.

Ayden spoke. "Everybody dead alive now?" It was a question.

The paw twitched in his hand.

"God no! The third wish." Nanni screamed.

The Mother's face blanched. She kept turning from Nanni to Ayden and moved back a few steps from the open door. Her husband's eyes on her made her feel like a cornered animal.

"Antoinette!" the son called out into the darkness, then he bolted outside.

Nanni was at the door. She saw many figures shambling on the road, but she could not recognize anyone. They were human silhouettes. Loud voices and wild shrieks came from neighboring houses. The road became more crowded as if a big parade were going by.

She called out her daughter's name, then threw herself into the mass of teeming bodies that continued to pour out from the earth.

In honor of W. W. Jacobs

Eddie The Great

Steve Rasnic Tem

The clerk at the dietary supplements store wore a tight yellow T-shirt, "Power Supplied," emblazoned in a large red, lightning-bolt font across the chest. The young fellow had an abundance of muscles, but something seemed odd about their configuration, as if he had been crudely sculpted by a child well-versed in comic books but with very little knowledge of human anatomy.

Eddie examined the huge keg in his hands, also labeled with the store brand. His own muscles trembled under the weight of it. "So this powder, it gives you the nutrients you can't get even with proper eating?"

"It's because of the way the environment has impacted our food supply." The clerk spoke eagerly, and a little too wide-eyed. "Even when you farm organically, the water, the air, even the soil, it's all been poisoned, and for so many generations we don't even recognize it as poison anymore. Don't get me started on what a joke the current EPA standards are."

Eddie had no intention to. "And this will help me build a great body?"

"A great body, a great mind, superior eyesight, and phenomenal emotional health as well. It's all yours—you just have to make a start, and stay with the program."

"How long?"

"With the proper exercise program and the right attitude I don't see why a gentleman of your age couldn't have miraculous results in two years, three tops."

"I'm only forty," Eddie said tersely.

"Oh, a great time to start!" The lad said, smiling, though his face looked scarlet with embarrassment.

Eddie looked the young man in the eye and asked, "What if I said that your two, three years was too long?"

"Well, Mister—"

"Call me Eddie. I want everybody to call me Eddie."

The fellow looked doubtful, and Eddie realized he was probably even younger than he appeared. "Well, it's just that good health takes time. It's like Mr. Boyer, my boss, says, 'it took you all your life to get out of shape—you can't undo that damage overnight.'"

"Very true, very true," Eddie grinned as if his question had been some kind of test. "But I've also heard that your Mr. Boyer has done a great deal of research in the area, and that he might have some special, um, formulations available? Some special product line available to customers with sufficient funds? I just wanted you to know, Mickey . . ."

The boy's face had reddened. "Sir, my name isn't . . ."

"... isn't Mickey, I know, I know, no offense. It's just that I am a very busy man, young whatever-your-name-is, and money really is no object. After all, good health is a priceless commodity—as I'm sure your Mr. Boyer would agree."

The clerk, still red-faced, walked away without saying another word. The man who replaced him was much older, much better built, but also seemed to have little to say. He simply stared at Eddie, his lips set into a narrow unyielding line splitting the middle of his massive jaw. There were no other customers—no doubt he could have handled the problem Eddie presented any way he wanted to. He watched while Eddie counted a large quantity of cash onto the counter, then studied Eddie's face for a discomfiting period of time. Finally he went into the backroom, returning with a case of unlabelled blue bottles and a typewritten sheet of instructions.

Eddie had never thought of himself as one of the geniuses, the ones who took instant grasp of any intellectual problem, immediately placing their own individual spin on it, even contributing some creative twist that increased the store of human knowledge. He was both in awe and frankly frightened of such people, and consequently disappointed and relieved not to be among them.

But you didn't have to be a genius in order for people to remember you. The formula for achieving fame was much more complicated, and harder to divine. And certainly the famous were possessed of a kind of divinity. Eddie did not pretend to understand the machinery of that divinity, but he had faith it could be learned, and that anything, including chance, could be manipulated toward that end.

Insisting that everyone call him "Eddie" had some obvious risks, the foremost being that some might not take him seriously. "Eddie" was the name of a kid, or a comedian. Eddie Cochran, Eddie Van Halen, Eddie Murphy, Eddie Munster. But he counted on its non-threatening quality, and its potential as a singular identifier. The world had had its Napoleon, its Einstein, its Madonna. He intended to deliver its Eddie.

Eddie opened one of the blue bottles and drank it on his way to acting class. It had an underlying citrus tang and a vinegary aftertaste. Nothing you'd want to be addicted to, but he thought he could tolerate it as long as it brought results.

In acting class Eddie's Henry V sounded more like Henry Kissinger, but a career in acting was not in his sights. What he wanted was simply to sound more sincere, to have people convinced that he really believed the things he said. It made them pay attention to you when you spoke, even when the actual content of your speech was plainly nonsensical.

He was thirsty after class as he often was—sincerity always seemed to dry out his mouth. He emptied the contents of another blue bottle down his throat but it didn't help any— it just created more gas. In the initial meeting with his new PR consultant he let her do most of the talking. She was a dark, curly-haired woman of some intensity, who seemed a bit off her stride when dealing with him. "It really doesn't matter what you do—business, politics, entertainment—I'll do a great job for you. But it would really, help," she said, looking a little hesitant, "if I knew more about *what* you do."

"I work for an insurance company," he stated, through the

beginnings of chest pain.

"Insurance," she repeated doubtfully.

"Yes, but that's not what I need you to publicize. I mean, who would want to publicize *that*," said through gritted teeth. "I need you for what comes *after*, for the things I'm *going* to do." He squeezed his eyes shut on the pain. Was he having a heart attack? Not now, not when he was on his way at last.

"Well, advanced preparation, that *can* help, especially if it's an involved campaign. So, exactly what do you have planned? Say—are you alright?" She put her hand on his arm, which made his skin burn so he brushed it away.

"Fine," he said, the discomfort making him growl. "Sorry, a little gas, that's all." He saw her frown, chose to ignore it. "My plan—is being planned right now, you know? I'll let you know when the plan is ready. But surely there are things you can do in preparation, right? I mean, I imagine the preliminaries are pretty much the same, whatever the job?"

"Well, we can take some photographs—I'll send you to my guy. And we can do some basic design work, typography, letterhead, that sort of thing.

"Great, great," he said, cutting her off and rising to his feet. "I'll call you," and then he left the room, ran down the stairs and out the door, quickly finding a cool brick wall to lean against, take comfort from.

It wasn't until he got into his car and stretched to roll the window down that he realized his chest had expanded somewhat, his arms bigger, tighter inside the thin cotton sleeves. He grinned deliciously, feeling all John Wayne, John the Baptist, John Belushi.

By the time he stopped at Tomorrow Digital Design he was

feeling tremendous, expansive. He approved the new website design, gave the little fellow with the unfortunate glasses the new PR contact information, gave him the go ahead to move forward with the social media plan, all details to be filled in later, of course. When he himself learned those details. He put his hand on the receptionist's lower back as he was leaving, and she did not stiffen. He rolled the top down on the new convertible for the ride home. Emily did not understand why he needed such an expensive automobile, but someday he would explain the plan to her, and with such powers of communication she would agree completely.

She was fixing dinner when he arrived, their boys in the backyard playing together like little animals—they'd come to the table later scratched and bleeding, but happy, eyes shiny with excitement. Eddie and his brother had been the same way.

He nibbled on her neck. She relaxed and sighed, then suddenly squirmed away. "Your work called," she said, not looking at him. "Apparently you weren't there today."

Eddie sighed, and when Emily wasn't looking stuck two fingers into the steaming pot of mashed potatoes, jammed them into his mouth still steaming. His eyes watered, but he made no sound. "So . . ." he said, drawing it out. "What did you tell them?"

"I told them you were too sick to get out of bed, too sick even to get on the phone. What else was I supposed to tell them?"

"It'll be okay." He sucked on his burnt fingers. "I work hard for them—there's no one else in the department with my experience level. They can afford for me to miss a Friday every now and then. I'm not their only employee that does that."

"I know you've got ambition, Eddie. And that you're doing work way below your potential. But it's not like we don't need your paycheck. Your side expenses alone—"

"—are an essential investment," he continued for her. "Not just for me, but for what I can eventually get for all of us."

"Honey, we don't need—"

"It's not about need. It's about deserve. I've been working on the plan every weekend, you know that, just figuring out the possibilities. Most people have about twenty years to become something, something other than what they started out as, and most people start out as nothing much at all—somebody's near-invisible kid, somebody's anonymous schoolmate, poor relation, or maybe that casual acquaintance whose name you can never remember. Not much at all. Less than nothing. That's not going to be me, and working in insurance isn't going to get me where I need to be."

"People have different ideas about success." As she began talking he noticed how very birdlike she was, had always been, with her narrow jaw, and pointy lips like a little curved beak, and with her hair swept back like that, she was just this perfect little bird, hardly even a mouthful, you'd barely even taste anything even if you ate her whole. "You can be a successful husband," she said, with that cute little beak. "You can be a successful father. That's what's really important."

He kept his hands deliberately away from her. A bird's bones were hollow, and extremely fragile. "And I don't want to minimize that, not in the least, but people say things like that, forgive me dear, when they just have no faith a man can be more than that. I'll be a great father, I *am* a great father, but I'm going to be lots more than that. I started late—most of the real success stories—the Bill Gateses, the Bill Haleys, Bill Clinton, Bill Bradley, Bill Blake, Bill Maher—they started young and kept working. I have to be exceptional, starting as late as I am. But you'll see, dear," he said, almost sneering, his mouth feeling strange, not quite his own, his teeth, his tongue not quite fitting, "you won't believe your eyes, all the things that you'll see."

He began his Saturday with the contents of two more blue bottles, followed by two hours of vigorous exercise, doubling and tripling his normal number of reps at each routine. Then at the end he could have worked that stationary bike all day, but he didn't have the time. He drank another blue bottle down and headed to his office in the basement, where he'd spent most of every Saturday for years, locked away, planning, figuring, invisible and oblivious to the rest of the world.

Plans and diagrams and dreams. Eddie obsessed over them, making them both occupation and preoccupation. Once he went through his office door (thick, barred, double-locked, the most secure door in the house) he was surrounded by the tools necessary to envision, develop, and achieve them—everything someone like him needed to become someone else. One wall was jammed with books on business, wealth-building, creative expression, how-to's and how-not-to's, and guides for everything from taxidermy to makeup to Astromechanics. On another wall he had created charts outlining the education and career development of Stephen Hawking, Toni Morrison, George Washington, Muammar Muhammad al-Gaddafi, James Baldwin, James Mason, James Thurber, King James, Etta James, and countless others. Another wall held tools both electronic and mechanical, antique and recent, musical and silent, complicated to construct and handmade simple. There was a mirror to practice body language and expression, a video camera for self observation, an artist's easel and a sculptor's wheel. Down here he had attempted to become a writer, a painter, an inventor, a ventriloquist, a musician, a magician and a mime. Nothing had quite clicked as yet, nothing had set off that complex chain reaction through which a star was born. But lack of complete success did not trouble him—as far as he knew he was training for something no one had even invented or imagined yet.

Every Saturday he locked himself inside this room, not even returning upstairs for meals, having brought a small supply of sandwiches and bottled water down with him. For the rest of the family this became "Dad's Invisible Day," and the children weren't allowed to speak to him, to break his concentration in any way, even if he ventured upstairs seeking additional supplies, food, or the bathroom. Emily had enforced the rule with the children early on, though a bit hesitantly at first, then as the years passed the practice became part of the fabric of their family life, never questioned and rarely even commented upon.

Today, however, today there was a great deal of agitation during Eddie's time in the basement. There had been agitation before—you could not focus such ambition, such yearning, such energy into one small space without there being some agitation, anxiety, a nervous display of high emotion. But today it seemed worst than it ever had been, resulting in bouts of aggressive pacing, and due to the cramped quarters a kind of winding occurred, a winding up, a coiling, a building up of incredible energy impatient for release.

As if attempting to quench a fire Eddie had taken to consuming more of the blue-bottled fluid, and although it continued to promise a certain satiation, that state was never quite reached, remaining always just of reach of teeth, tongue, and desire. In fact his teeth and tongue continued to feel ill-fitting, increasingly alien in his mouth, and when he went to the mirror, opening his mouth so impossibly wide that he imagined his entire head must be hinged around it, and that if he wasn't careful the back of his head might collide viciously with his spine, he saw that his teeth had expanded, become both more numerous and twice as wide as they had been, and his tongue as wide and as loose as a pennant down the cavern of his throat.Something also had happened to Eddie's hearing. His ears rang, as if over-stimulated, as if full. It was difficult to pick out an individual sound that annoyed him—the entirety, the soup of sound had become excruciating. But over time the individual threads of annoyance separated out, and he discovered that the sound of his watch's internal electronics was more than he could bear, and took it off, and crushed it under his heel. And then there was that tinny clamor, that munchkin squeal of quarreling monkeys, and god knows where their mother was, who'd promised, who'd *promised*, they wouldn't disturb him.

He was through his office door and up the basement stairs and rushing into the back yard before he'd even realized what he was about to do, his thoughts consumed by a painful white heat. He stretched out his hands—amazed at the reach of them, the length and thickness of his fingers, like sausages, like tree limbs, the incredible breadth of his palms—and knocked his little boys out of their perches on the jungle gym. They tumbled giggling, believing this was all a joke, that Daddy was playing monster again, snapping and growling, but Eddie knew it wasn't play, and that the growls, the inarticulate snaps his jowls and lips were making, were involuntary, and not pretense at all.

"Daddeee!" He stopped, looking down at Liz, his Elizabeth, his youngest, as she cowered on the ground at his feet, consumed by his dark shadow, which appeared so impossibly swollen, so immense and ill-proportioned.

He dropped down slowly, collapsing into himself, sprawling loosely on the ground beside his shuddering child. "Oh, Liz," he said. "Liz, Liz, Lizzie," he repeated, thinking about how small she was, and how appallingly mortal. "You'll live forever, my Lizzie," he lied. "Like all the great legends. Liz Taylor, Elizabeth I, Elizabeth Bishop, Liz, Elizabeth Browning, Liz Lizzie Borden, Liz, look at Daddy, please don't cry."

Eddie left work early Monday morning to get to an appointment downtown at the offices of Unlimited Potential. They never called what they did hypnotism. Instead they used phrases like "subconscious query" and "cognitive therapeutic sleep." Not that he cared, as long as the job got done, and he arrived at who he needed to be. Everyone had the right of renaming, he supposed.

He finished off his last blue bottle downstairs in the parking lot before going in. He tried not to panic. But what if he couldn't get a new supply? And what if he ran out again? It wasn't right that he might be denied his journey for lack of a few bottles of the right lubricant.

"When last we left off you were talking about your goals." When Eddie had first met the counselor her youth had put him off—she looked barely out of college. But she proved to be a quick study. Besides, the world belonged now to people her age—who better to help him conquer it?

"I didn't use the word goals. That's a defeatist term, in my opinion. If you call them goals you leave open the possibility, by definition, that you might not achieve them. These are *requirements*, have-to's. Failure is not an option."

"But let us just suppose, for argument's sake, that you did *not* achieve them—what would you do then?"

"No, no argument about it." He grinned broadly at her, but it wasn't sincere. "Can't happen. If you leave that door to self-doubt open, even just a crack, you're done for."

"I see. So why are these requirements so important to you?"

He felt a violent rush of impatience. He couldn't understand why she insisted on droning on like this—why couldn't she get on to the hypnosis, or the therapeutic sleep, or whatever they wanted to call it? That's why he'd been coming here. That last drink from the blue bottle had fatigued him—he could barely hold his eyes open. All that stimulus—eventually you had to pay the price. "Look," he said, grinding his teeth, which were so large now it felt like he had a mouth full of marbles. "*Look*. I'm forty years old now. Next month I'll be forty-one. Do you think they give you much time to make a name for yourself in this world?" He answered for her. "They do not. And some would say, *some*, that I'm already well past my prime. I would do *anything* to become who I'm supposed to be. *Anything.* I'm a *shy* person, I always have been. But not where this is concerned. Where this is concerned I would scream from the rooftops, eat live chickens like one of those geeks in the old sideshows. Do you think that embarrasses me? That does not. At the end of the day you're just as dead, whatever you've done to get there."

"Eddie? Eddie, are you all right?"

"Well, of course I'm all right! I'm still alive—how much righter could I be?"

"Your chest . . . your arm."

He looked down at himself. Part of his chest, the portion roughly over his heart, had swollen to three, four times its normal size. The swelling had spread to his left arm, his biceps ballooning, his best sports jacket and the shirt underneath, beginning to split from the pressure. He looked directly at her and grinned his patented Eddie grin. "I've been working out, you know? That's self-actualization in action, baby!"

"Should I call someone?" She looked so uncomfortable, so awkward sitting there in her women's pin-striped business attire. It was to laugh. Maybe she wanted to kiss him, maybe she really wanted to lay one on him—maybe that was why she was so uncomfortable.

"No, no it's okay, sweetheart. Never you mind. You have to understand, most people, they want to be someone else, they would just *love* to be someone else, but the problem is most people are toadies—they're followers. They're too damned scared to go out and *seek* what they want to be. Instead they *hide* inside themselves. They cower. They hide when they should be seeking, get it? Hide and seek, it's humanity's game, and most of us are losing that game, big time." He said that last bit rather calmly, he thought, but at the end of it he reached over and broke the corner off the counselor's heavy oak desk. He hadn't really intended to—he supposed he just didn't know his own strength. He grinned at her charmingly and showed her the piece.

He called Emily and told her he'd be working late. "Eddie, the mortgage check? It bounced! Do you know anything about that?"

"I haven't the time to talk about that now, Emily. I don't know—there must have been insufficient funds."

"But *why* wasn't there enough in there to cover it?"

"I don't know, expenses, I guess. Don't worry about it—it'll be taken care of."

"What have you been spending *our money* on, Eddie?"

"I told you! Expenses! It costs a lot of money to succeed in this world! But it's an *investment*, can't you understand that much? It'll be *okay*. Once my plan rolls out we'll be *drowning* in money—we'll get a much bigger house. *Don't worry*." He hung up.

Eddie drove to a truck rental company a mile or so from Power Supplied, renting one he thought would probably be big enough for what he had in mind. If not, he'd just make two trips. He pulled up in the alley behind the store and started beating on the steel door in the back wall. He beat as hard as he could for a very long time, and it didn't hurt his hand at all. In fact his hand made a rather satisfying dent in the metal.

Finally the owner, looking fresh and splendid in his bright yellow and red tee, came and opened the door. Eddie pushed his way inside, Mister Muscles unable to stop him.

The oh-so-reluctant proprietor didn't want to sell the stuff to him, but Eddie had a big sack full of money from their now-depleted bank account, and he was very insistent. The fellow even helped young Mickey the clerk load the truck, before leaving with a somewhat disgusted look on his face.

Before Eddie drove off the clerk passed his receipt through the window, his hand trembling. "Good deal," Eddie said. "Who knows, maybe getting to the new me will be a tax-deductible journey?" He tossed his paperwork on the seat beside him and flashed the young man his best, his hungriest, his toothiest Eddie grin.

The clerk stepped back. "Mister," he said. "I really shouldn't say anything, but this supplement, it's really . . . nothing special. I mean it's healthy enough—it's loaded with vitamins and sea weed extract and protein additives, and all kinds of enzymes."

"Sounds like a *power supplier* sure enough!" Eddie declared, his extreme grin beginning to hurt his face, but he figured no pain no gain in any case so no problem there.

"But there are a lot of products out there with pretty much the same stuff in them, only cheaper. Mister Boyer, he's no crook, but a lot of what you're paying for, it's the blue bottles— he orders them special."

"Well, I do like *bluuuu*," Eddie crooned.

The clerk shook his head. "But it's just a *supplement*, a vitamin, juice, and enzyme cocktail. Boyer, he oversells it, makes it seem all mysterious and forbidden, that's why he keeps it under the counter, or in the back room. But there's nothing *magic* about it."

"Kid, let me tell you something. Remember how you told me that you needed the right attitude?"

"And exercise—I also said exercise."

"Yeah yeah. But the attitude part? Kid, I've got that in *spades*. And this." He held up his arm, which pulsed visibly, pumping so much blood into his hand the hand had gone purple. The kid stumbled back. And Eddie drove off in a cloud of smoke, enveloped in the happy sound of rattling bottles.

He got back to the house late—the kids were probably already in bed, but the light was still on in his and Emily's bedroom. Emily liked to read at night, and Eddie approved—anything that might improve her—it might help her appreciate his own quest. If she only better understood the sacrifices he'd made for this family, and still continued to make, she might be a bit more supportive.

It took him a while to unload the truck. Good thing that he'd been working out. Even better thing that he'd been drinking all that pretty liquid blue. That kid back at the store was obviously envious, probably worked there all this time thinking his boss would let him in on the secret, and now Eddie comes in, lays down the cash, and takes it all away. He didn't blame the kid, but Eddie had himself to think about. And his family. Besides, Eddie was obviously genetically predisposed to benefit the most from whatever formula had been used in this blue brew. Some people were just born with physical and chemical advantages. Maybe that wasn't fair, but it really couldn't be helped—such was the way of the world. When Eddie fully became, he knew he'd encounter a lot of envy, a lot of sabotage. He was going to have to become extra vigilant.

But Emily wasn't reading. He caught her red-handed, packing a suitcase.

"What's this?"

She twisted her tiny bird head around, startled, pecking at the air the way startled birds will. "Your boss called. They've fired you. He was nice enough, but he said you've missed just too many days."

"Huh!" He put his hands on his hips dramatically. "How about *that*! That bastard!"

"Ed, how *could* you?"

"Hey — " He waved his forefinger at her. He wasn't positive, but he thought that finger was a lot longer than it used to be. "I *told* you—it's *Eddie* now."

"I always trusted you—Eddie. I must have been a *fool*!"

"No, no, we're all fools, little bird, until we decide to do something about our lives. Until we stop being prey, or road kill, and climb into that driver's seat, and become old-fashioned predators again, meat-eaters."

"Ed—Eddie, you need help." She turned her back on him, continuing to pack as if he weren't even there. He gingerly put out his hand, cautious of his new strength, and gently cupped her shoulder with it. And still the little bird shrugged herself away from him, as if his touch meant nothing to her.

"Listen to me!" He spun her around, and although he felt some pain in a distant part of his brain from the shocked look on her face he didn't let it deter him. He sat her down forcefully on the edge of the bed, making her bounce a little, which made him squeeze her arms just a little tighter because he was afraid she might fall off the bed and hurt herself. Her face went pale and she closed her eyes. Now afraid she was going to pass out, he shook her. Her head bounced around to a frightening degree.

"Listen, just listen," he ordered softly, and knelt on the floor in front of her. He was obviously much taller than he used to be, and she was obviously much smaller. She looked dazed, little bird caught in some steel-jawed trap. "I just want this family to be the most it can be."

He relaxed his hands somewhat, and instead tried to hold her still with his eyes, which he understood now to be enormous, luminous, unforgettable.

"It started with me, but I can help you, too. Then later we can extend the benefits to the kids, make them so superior none of their classmates will be able to even touch them.

"Surely there's someone you've always wanted to be? Emily Blunt, Emily Dickinson, Emily Bronte, maybe Emily Post? We can make that happen. Did you know there are exercises, supplements, advanced techniques now, that can make you someone else? Reach your potential? I can *help* you, and the kids. I really can."

But she was crying. Not loudly. The tears were simply leaking out of her, like ice, sweating. "I don't want to be someone else," she said, her little bird body trembling all over.

"Well, *fine!*" He leapt to his feet. He'd inadvertently dragged her to her feet as well. He let go and she collapsed on the bed like a frail old person. "That's just *great*. Wait right there—we're going to have a family meeting right *now*."

Eddie locked the bedroom door behind him, pounded

down the stairs to the boys' bedroom, scooped them up one under each arm and strode across the hall to Liz's. He shifted one of the boys to his shoulder—he wasn't sure which one—but the kid was half giggling, half asleep. Eddie pulled Liz, who still hadn't stirred, close to his chest, and headed back upstairs.

With his family arranged on the bed in front of him—Liz still asleep, one of the boys rubbing the sleep out of his eyes, the other staring at Eddie wide-eyed while clutching his mom, who still looked out of it, like some sort of crazed deranged person—Eddie began to pace back and forth.

"I've got a plan for this family." He wanted to look serious about it, but unable to keep the grin out of his face, "not just some idle thoughts, but a carefully-thought-out, scientifically reasonable plan. It may be too late for your mother—sometimes as we get older we get too set in our ways—but you kids, you can reap the most benefit out of this plan. I promise you, you just listen to me and follow this plan and someday you'll have everything you ever wanted out of life."

One of the boys said, "Toys?"

Eddie threw back his head, dropped open his mouth, and brayed so long and loud it made his head hurt. Then he looked down at the boy, who looked surprised, or scared—it was hard to tell which.

"Oh I *promise* you," Eddie declared, "there will be *lots* of toys!" He started pacing again. "Now, most people, *most people*," he said, looking at Emily, "they live their lives waiting for things to happen. Good or bad it doesn't matter—they have no control over it. They spend their time daydreaming about what they might have been, and then they die, with all those dreams, that potential, wasted.

"Now, I'm not pointing any fingers, kids. After all, most of the human race is like that. And I don't want to see you kids pointing any fingers, either. You have to be respectful. You have to feel sorry for people like that.

"But I want better for my family. I don't want the members of *my* family to die unknown, like they were nothing more than dumb cattle. I want each of you to become famous, celebrities—the people all those other anonymous people spend all their days reading about, envying. Do you know what celebrities are in this world, boys and girls? They're divine. They're gods—people read about them the way some people read the bible."

Emily had been lying on the bed through all this, her face toward the ceiling. Eddie had thought her passed out, sleeping, or maybe even dead. But now she spoke up, still not showing him the respect of looking at him while she was talking, but at least she was talking. "Okay, okay, Eddie. So where's this plan? At least we should find out what we're in for."

He wasn't expecting this. "Well, sure, I guess it's about time. I just have to put it together into some kind of format the rest of you can digest. Print it out, or something."

"Come on, Eddie, quit stalling. We all want to see your glorious plan."

She didn't *really* want to see the plan. She was just trying to get his goat. Well, consider it got. "Come on, then!" he cried, sweeping his arms in melodramatic enthusiasm. "I'll take you down to the office, show you around! I'm not going to need it anymore, anyway. From now on we share, and this entire house will be *our office*!

The kids cried because he was herding them so hard on the steps and they couldn't keep up. Emily looked wide awake now, alarmingly alert, as if she had been sneaking sips from one of his blue bottles. She'd better not be. If he ever found out she had, he'd be obliged to deal with her harshly.

They piled into his office, and suddenly this cozy space in which he had spent some of the most important time in his life seemed unbearably cramped, with all of them packed in there, as if he couldn't possibly find room for them all in his plan, in his life, and quite possibly at least one of them would have to go.

His skin prickled as he saw his children touching his things, laying their grubby hands on the charts and diagrams and schemes posted on his walls. Elizabeth picked up one of the old dusty books from a pile of them on the floor and he really thought he might scream.

"Neat, Dad," one of them said, although he couldn't remember the name, or recognize the face. In his anxiety he grabbed one of the blue bottles piled haphazardly across his desk, snapped the cap open on his teeth, and chugged it.

"Is it in your 'puter?" Lizzie said, and he made himself smile.

"Yeah . . . yeah." He sat down at the keyboard, sweeping stacks of papers and books off his desk onto the floor with a swing of his pulsing, warping, agonizing arm. His fingers were obviously much bigger than they had been the day before, which made typing difficult, but not impossible. After a few attempts he managed to get his user name and password in, and then he saw the folders—Plan 1, Plan 2, Plan for Next Year, Backup Plan, and so forth, and began opening them one at a time, peeking at the individual files randomly, and then with furious thoroughness, as file after file appeared to be blank, or full of gibberish, or consisted of apparently random words and images copied from various internet sites, the only coherence a relatively consistent color palette of reds and purples and patterns stimulating to a primitive and bestial eye.

"Who! Who!" He couldn't quite find the words, even as the sheer volume of the sounds he was making grew louder.

"Ed! Calm down!" Emily had her hands on his shoulders. What did she want? Her fingertips were scalding!

"Eddie! It's Eddie, you bitch! Who's been down here? Who's been in my computer, erasing me? Erasing every bit of me!"

"Ed—Eddie, *no* one! No one's been in here!"

"Lie to me! You all would lie to me!" He felt himself rising, his head expanding, his shoulders, his muscles, all rising into perfection, into bliss. "I will show you! Show you!" he bellowed, did Eddie, Eddie the shark, Eddie the sixth, Eddie the great, the great Eddie Hyde, as Emily struck him from behind, and struck him again, yet again, and he could almost admire her spirit, almost rejoice in her transformation, as his mind went as brilliant, and white, and blank as his plans.

In honor of Robert Louis Stevenson's
Strange Case of Dr Jekyll and Mr Hyde

A True Blue Bouquet

Ivan Fanti

A belardo leaves the bar and is some streets away when
he pukes in the gutter. The tequila was cheap, obviously
tainted, and the women in the bar did not care for college students with empty pockets. One woman wore a hat with a pea-
cock feather. A dark eye in the feather clearly stared at him
all night while the woman did not once glance in his direction.
He knows he will dream about women tonight.

He heads home hoping his landlady is not awake to see
him coming in and ask again for the overdue rent. He had
spent too much in the bar. Like many young men, Abelardo
lets himself be dragged through life by his weaknesses.

He has not noticed that the man in the palm sombrero has
been following him since he left the bar. When he straightens

his lean body up from the gutter, the first thing Abelardo sees is a long machete.

"Don't move, señor, or you're dead."

"What do you want? I have no money."

"I spit on your money. I just want your eyes."

"What…? What are you talking about?"

"My woman wants a bouquet of blue eyes. You have blond hair, so you must have blue eyes, too. Don't lie to me – you are not the first person I've approached this night and it is late."

"My hair color is from bleach; I was not born with it."

"Don't try to fool me, señor," the man with the machete says harshly, "I will have my bouquet."

"For the love of Jesu…"

"Don't talk to me of our Lord. Let me see your eyes."

Abelardo covers his face with his elbow. The man with the machete grabs Abelardo's arm and drags him into the vestibule of a closed barber shop where a neon sign illuminates the doorway. Abelardo hasn't been near a barber shop in a long time. The dim light gives a greenish cast to the scene. The man holds the machete high and pulls Abelardo's face close to his own.

"Open your eyes or I'll cut off your lids."

Abelardo does as the man instructs and can only see the blackness of the machete blade.

"They look blue to me."

Abelardo's heart quickens. "No, they are gray. You are making a mistake."

"They will have to do, señor. The dawn will be here soon and I can't go back without my bouquet. If your hair color is fake, then who knows what color your eyes are. I know about contact lenses."

"How will your sweetheart feel if you give her a gray bouquet?" Abelardo asks him.

"It will be worse if I return with empty hands. I'm sorry, señor," the man says in a soft voice that sounds almost embarrassed.

The voice gives Abelardo no comfort. The blade comes closer to his eyes and a lock of blond hair comes down over his forehead. Something in the stranger's hard face, bathed in the greenish light, gives him an idea.

"Wait! I have a solution to your problem."

The man holds his hand steady.

"My landlady's cat has green eyes. It would be better than my dull gray eyes – you can see that, can't you? – and your soul will still be mostly pure in our Lord's eyes."

"A cat's eye is more beautiful than a man's. My woman would like that. Green, you say… that is rare around here. Where is this cat?"

"The rooming house is not far."

He seems to be thinking and eventually grunts and nods. "Which way, señor?" is all he says.

Abelardo glances once in a while at the man trailing him, just to see if the distance between them is enough for him to break into a mad run. They walk without conversation.

I'm not proud of what I did that night. I used matches to sneak around the rooming house in the dark. The cat made no sound, being of a gentle, trusting nature. The silence of the house was filled only with my heartbeat.

"Yes, it's as you said, they are green." The man held onto the feline tightly. "But I think I will need something else in case my woman should not be pleased."

Weakly, I watched the man with the palm sombrero and machete walk off carrying the cat. The next day the landlady was more concerned with finding her pet than inquiring after her rent or wondering where all my hair had gone. And so it was that paper notices for a lost cat appeared on walls and lamp posts all over the neighborhood. I saw many of them at the university dormitory when I finally moved out of the rooming house a week after the incident. My hair would grow back and I will leave it its natural dark color. I like to believe that the cat with green eyes now has a new owner with blond hair.

In honor of Octavio Paz

Ghostless

Paul Di Filippo

I think that every Starbucks in the world together consti-
tute the saddest place on earth. These ubiquitous shops
form one big nexus of sorrow, grief, misery, pain, regret and
weltschmerz, packetized and distributed globally. Why do I
say this?

1) The staff doesn't want to be there.

2) Everything is overpriced.

3) The customers know and resent 1) and 2).

4) The furnishings represent your own parlor if it had been
designed by a committee of dead faux beatniks, and the mer-

maid logo gets steadily less sexier with every iteration.

5) The customers are all in a hurry, except for the ones who have no lives and nothing else to do.

6) The customers are made to feel guilty if they patronize any other coffee shop.

7) When they are not feeling guilty, they are inclined to feel superior.

8) Everyone listens to everyone else's private conversations.

9) The befouled toilets are always occupied.

10) Not one soulless Starbucks ever sprang up spontaneously to meet a need or a dream; they are all calculated investments.

These conditions breed and attract sadness like Russian prisons breed TB.

That's why I hang out there.

It's how I find the people who need my services.

The name I use these days is Ilona Myfawny, and I'm a matchmaker.

Today I had a wide selection of potential clients.

It was six o'clock on a winter's evening. Thin, dingy rain spat and drizzled past the lighted street lamps on the far side of the windows. The pavements shone long and sodium-white.

My venue was the Starbucks at NYU, on the southeast corner of Washington Square. Talk about ironic, right? A Starbucks located smack dab in the original American birthplace of coffeehouse culture. I find that the implicit irony lures patrons who are even more despondent than the usual run of customers at other branches. Although the extra-high ceiling and ornate white columns of the interior here do offset the claustrophobic, harshly lit prison vibe a tad. But on the whole, the equation is in my favor. Plus, the place is close to my own apartment.

A petite blonde woman—dressed in H&M from head to toe and sitting alone with her back to the wall, crossed leg nervously jigging—compulsively tickled and stroked her smartphone, as if to cause it to jet out a desperate jackpot of hope like some tiny slot machine. Two male students hashed out their grim post-graduation prospects with the raw blind vigor of hyenas apportioning a carcass. A teaching assistant graded an infinite stack of exams like Sisyphus working his way up a vertical slope. An unshaven boho wannabe writer, hands poised over laptop keyboard, sought blank-eyed inspiration in a poster advertising the latest release from Putamayo. Like gas escaping from a fat dirigible, a levi'd professor spouted off to a small coterie of smug ragged sycophants about how to fix the nation's foreign policy. Two suits wearing the men inside them exchanged ticker-tape stock market factoids like robots on a car assembly line handing off unfinished engine blocks for reaming.

I shook my head wearily, to snap out of my own funk. Sometimes the quiet desperation of my clients got to me. I couldn't afford to grow callous or cynical. I had to keep my empathy fine-tuned and broadband. Otherwise, I'd never succeed in placing anyone with their perfect match.

Across my own table I saw now a seated man. I knew him instantly as Captain Howard Updegrove, a former tugboat operator who had guided big liners into their docks on the Hudson, before his retirement. With his peacoat'd barrel torso, thick beard and wild thatchroof of hair, he resembled a bear dressed up in human clothes.

I ostentatiously put my phone on the table between me and the Captain, and adjusted my cordless headset. The phone registered no caller, but no one else needed to know that, so long as I seemed to be talking through it to someone.

"Hello, Captain Updegrove. How are you feeling?"

The Captain looked bemused. "Just fine—I suppose. Where are we?"

"A coffee house in Greenwich Village."

"Where are all the flappers?"

"Scant on the ground nowadays, Captain. I take it you've been dispossesed just recently."

"Yes, yes—Alex died this morning. Without him, there was no point in staying in the apartment."

"So you need a new home."

"I suppose so."

"See anyone here you fancy?"

The Captain looked around critically. "Not really, no."

"Well, let's just hang out a while then. I'm sure someone will turn up."

"'Hang out?'"

"Relax."

"Oh."

I stood up and pocketed my phone. "I'm just going to get myself a drink."

I didn't offer to buy the Captain anything, and he seemed content.

No one sat down at my table while I waited on line, although once or twice people hesitated over its availability. The Captain didn't bother with them.

I spent so much time at Starbucks, I had to go easy on the caffeine. Back at the table with a Peppermint Hot Chocolate, I kept my eye on the door.

A dozen customers came and went before a likely candidate entered. Although I registered the man's significance and suitability immediately, the Captain took no notice of him. But that was typical. The average person so seldom recognized who would make a good partner. That judgment took an expert such as myself.

The guy wore unexceptional clothes: grey corduroy pants, a brown Eddie Bauer barncoat over a checked shirt. Rugged face. His salt-and-pepper hair was buzzed short. I watched him order a tall latte, then take a chair. While he sipped it, he looked ready to cry.

Eventually Barncoat got up to leave. I waited three seconds after he got through the door, then said to the Captain, "Let's go."

The Captain obligingly followed me outside.

Barncoat was heading north. We lagged always a few yards behind him. The lousy weather had lessened the pedestrian traffic somewhat. I saw the sodden, blown scourings and street-wash of Manhattan, papers, rags, dregs, rinds, cigarette butts, sheets of bubblewrap, flap, float, and cringe along the gutters, hearing the sneeze and rattle of the bony subway through the sidewalk gratings.

Barncoat stopped at a newsstand and bought a package of gum and a sports magazine. So far, so good. I had had him pegged for a candybar purchase, but gum was close enough. He stopped outside a jewelry store and eyed the contents of the window as if seeing the bracelets and necklaces and rings worn by a numinous woman of his dreams. I had thought he'd zero in on a clothing store, so no bullseye, but good enough again.

On Waverly Place he let himself into Number 122, a nice brownstone and brick multi-unit townhouse.

The Captain and I waited outside in the light winter mist just long enough to give Barncoat a chance to get inside his apartment.

"Do you see him, Captain Updegrove?"

The Captain's eyes had gone unfocused, like pools of opalescent smoke. "Yes, he's sitting on a couch. He has a little box with buttons in his hand. He's poking the buttons. There's light and sound coming from some kind of radio device."

"Jesus, Captain, didn't Alex have a TV?"

"Alex only cared to read. I was with him for many years."

"Well, is TV a dealbreaker?"

"No, I used to like the movies. Chaplin especially."

"Good. What can you sense about our man?"

"His name is—is Bob. Bob Hazel. He works on a boat— the ferry to Liberty Island!"

I hadn't heard the Captain excited yet, and was gratified now to catch the tremor of tentative connection in his voice. That meant I was doing my job well.

"Bob isn't watching his TV anymore. He's bending forward and hanging his head between his knees. I do believe he's sobbing like a baby."

"Okay, Cap, that's your cue. Go to him now. Happy harbors!"

Captain Updegrove lightly ascended the stoop and passed through the door of 122 Waverly place without opening it, and, suffused with the sense of serenity and peace that always came with a match, I was alone,.

As alone as I ever get in a city full of ghosts.

Five years ago, I had been majoring in Computational Science at the Stevens Insititute of Technology in Hoboken, a nice boring young woman who had no aspirations other than maybe to optimize Amazon's recommendation algorithms. The most exciting thing that had ever happened to me was when, as a teenager, I won a free trip to Disney World. Years later I would wryly recall how much I had enjoyed the Haunted Mansion.

Then, in my senior year at Stevens, I turned twenty-one and began to hear sourceless voices. I knew schizophrenia often set in around that age, and I was convinced I had the disease.

I was too scared to see a doctor or talk to my folks. So I read everything about schizophrenia that I could find online. That was when I noticed something odd and asymptomatic.

The voices I heard weren't threatening or paranoid. Their talk didn't even relate to me. No one was ordering me to do something self-destructive or dangerous. It was all mild persiflage about other people, people I didn't even know. Almost like bland gossip in some celestial chatroom.

And then I began to see the origin of the voices, waveringly at first, then with more and more solidity, and I gradually realized and admitted, after a long period of denial, that I had ghosts instead.

I'm not sure I wouldn't rather have gone with schizophrenia. At least science has a medicine for that, and people comprehend your condition.

But rather, both reassuringly and dismayingly, I had suddenly become a sensitive, a medium, a channeler, a speaker to the dead.

Looking as solid as you or me, but imperceptible to anyone else, the ghosts would manifest to me unpredictably, anywhere, at any time. I might be in the campus library, on the toilet, in the shower, in a theater, attending class, riding the subway in Manhattan—and suddenly, I'd have ghostly company, ectoplasmic presences tagging along like Mary's little lamb.

The ghosts all seemed to be idealized versions of their living selves, or sampled composites drawn from points along their timelines. There were no drowned or burned or starved or shot or stabbed or hanged or poisoned or partially eaten or nursing-home-attenuated men and women. The ghosts mostly presented themselves as mature and vital adults. Not to say they were without their eerie qualities.

A flat, long girl, snivelling. A silent man and woman, dressed in black and carrying wreaths. A young man with a handsome, nasty face. A woman with gold hair and two gold teeth in front. A round, friendly owlish housewife in an apron and bearing a knife..

But I can't neglect the kids. There were lots of kids, of various ages. Dying young, they had no adult personas to display.

I remember one baby in a phantom stroller, with such an

ancient face…

When the ghosts finally materialized to me, I immediately tried talking to them, asking them what they wanted, and why me? But they seemed unable to hear me. The communication was all one-way.

The next few months were very frustrating, maddening even. I had no relief from the ghosts. They attended me around the clock, coming and going and returning without pattern, a swarm of inconsiderate hanger-on houseguests murmuring their idle complaints and observations and reminiscences, ignoring me and each other. I tried to tune out their presence, and often succeeded, when focused on one task or another. But then in a moment of failed mental discipline I would become aware of the lurking crowd again, and start to freak out. Sometimes I would awaken with a start in the night, flip on my bedlamp and see them standing patiently by my bed. (No, they didn't glow in the dark!)

My academic and social life started to go down the tubes. I certainly would have been driven truly insane if my relations with the ghosts hadn't changed.

And the change was all due to Corky.

Corky was a girl ghost, about twelve years old. She looked like the quintessential tomboy out of some Beverly Cleary novel: pigtails, bib overalls and hightop sneakers. She liked to talk about swimming and climbing trees and catching tadpoles and the teasing she endured from boys at school. She never mentioned technology or pop stars or shopping, so I knew she had to have lived a long time ago. In some strange way she reminded me of my own girlhood, even though my own youth had been so different, a blend of bad Eighties sitcom reruns and videogames, hair metal bands and BASIC programming. How did I know her name was Corky? She never uttered it, I realized after a while, but somehow I just *knew*. That was the first sign of some deeper bond between us not present with the other ghosts.

So one day Corky strolled alongside me, occasionally hopping and skipping and prancing ahead of me, as I walked through the streets of Hoboken on some forgotten errand. No other ghosts chanced to be around.

Suddenly desperate, I turned to the girl, not caring who was witnessing a crazy woman talking to no one, and said, "Corky, what do you want? How can I help you?"

She didn't seem to hear me, and her next words were an excited non-sequitur about building a tree fort.

Just then I came abreast of a woman about my own age, stylishly dressed, standing in front of The Brass Rail on Washington Street, and I was nearly knocked down by a shock of recognition.

I could sense this woman's innate sadness, her disquiet and dissatisfaction and worry and angst, as plainly as if it were written on a sandwich board strapped across her shoulders.

And somehow I knew that Corky could help her—was meant for her.

Corky appeared to register something too. She ceased her chattering, and looked at the woman with interest.

Was there a connection here? I had to be sure.

So we began following the stranger.

For the next six hours or so.

I observed the woman have lunch, get a pedicure, shop, have dinner, watch a movie at the Clearview, all before she finally ended up back home, where I was left standing outside in the twilight.

And that was when Corky began to directly address me.

"I can see what's she doing now. She has an old purse, and she's looking through it. It was her mother's. There's a driver's license, and some dried-up lipstick, a roll of mints and a brooch and a handkerchief with some initials embroidered on it."

"Corky—would you like to live with this person?"

The ghost regarded me with adolescent ingenuousness. "Do you really think I could?"

"I do! Go to her now!"

Corky slid sidewise through a wall and vanished.

And she never came back.

After that, I could talk to any ghost and they'd hear me.

So this is what I eventually pieced together.

Ghosts are drawn to sadness.

But they alleviate it! They don't cause sadness or enhance it, they palliate it!

Even though the people they "haunt" might never know they are haunted, the presence of a ghost in their lives adds a kind of reassuring spiritual dimension to their existence, and lightens their troubles.

And the ghosts get some kind of satisfaction as well from such relationships.

The ghosts who attended me were the untethered ones. They had lost their mortal counterparts through death of their living anchors and now drifted without companionship. I could sense their imploring subtext now.

And I could match them up with new, ghostless hosts!

That was my talent! (The ghosts themselves seemed unable to efficiently zero in on a new host, relying on chance and circumstance to meet one.) And every ghost I paired with a human would be one less to bother me.

I dropped out of school almost immediately, and began my new career.

What did I use for money? I certainly wasn't rich before my change.

Ghosts know some amazing things. You'd be surprised at how many buried coffee cans full of Seated Liberty Silver Dollars there are around, or unclaimed bank accounts. Accessing some of these resources bordered on the shady, so I had to adopt several different identities. Enter "Ilona Myfawny." My Computational Science studies had not been in vain after all, when it came to hacking.

Matchmaker to ghosts and mortals.

What a way to make a living!

I often switched my practice from one Starbucks to another, on a random basis. A lot of what I did involved intuition. I would get a feeling that the mate for a certain ghost who had been urgently troubling me could be found in a certain neighborhood, and off I'd go. Curiously enough, the ghosts that utilized my services seemed always to end up with humans from the five boroughs. Only once did I have to travel even as far as Teaneck to make a connection.

I had no explanation for these geographic quirks of my

profession. I assumed that any particular ghost could attach itself satisfactorily to any member of a select subset of humanity, and that any individual human could host any ghost who shared certain qualities. In other words, I was facilitating connections between classes of beings, not between perfect unique soul-mates. If those had been my parameters, my task would have been nigh impossible. Even as matters stood, vetting the human partner involved hours of tedious trailing and snooping, legwork and voyeurism

Still, I often speculated about trying to take one of my East Coast ghosts to California or Bombay or London—assuming they'd follow me so far—and seeing if I could conjure up a connection. Some day, maybe, when I wasn't so busy dealing with the needs of these spirits. (And when, exactly, might that be? The supply of ghosts and sad people seemed endless. After five years of this, I could easily foresee weariness and burnout on the horizon.)

Today I was trying to match up a ghost who scared me a little, and we were sitting in the Starbucks where Amsterdam crossed Broadway, a little below 71st Street.

Billy Burdekin, I knew for a fact, had not been a pleasant or likable human being. But I had to leave his criminal rap-sheet out of the mental equation, if I were to do my job.

He presented as pimply-faced young white guy of about twenty-five, affirming my knowledge of his youthful death. His invariant ghostly clothes consisted of a backwards ball cap, sports jersey, sag-assed shorts and pricey kicks. His neck sported crude runic tattoos, a decorative body-mod that always creeped me out, raising images in my mind of brawny convicts with razor blades and a paper cup of graphite paste scraped off a pencil. Billy's spectral badinage featured an F-bomb every other word.

These qualities explained why I was devoting so much effort to getting him off my hands. I really didn't want Billy Burdekin in my life anymore.

Nursing my White Chocolate Mocha Latte, I anxiously awaited the arrival of someone to adopt Billy.

"Fuck this shit," said Billy, apropros of nothing special.

"Yes, Mr. Burdekin, I too grow bored. But let us cultivate patience and civility."

"Suck my dick, bitch."

I sighed deeply, and slugged some more coffee.

Night came calling, and December rain began to bucket down, more granular slurry than otherwise.

A sodden homeless guy dripped into the shop, and I knew instantly. This was Billy's host.

The homeless man shook water off like a ragged dog, and dumped his string-tied, plastic-bag-wrapped parcels in a corner. The staff seemed used to him, and said nothing objectionable against him. He went to use the toilet.

"Get ready to move out, Billy."

"Eat shit and die."

"You already did, Billy."

When Homeless Guy returned from the john, he did not immediately leave. I shouldn't have been surprised. The weather continued miserable. Instead, he rummaged up enough change for a small house-blend coffee and took it to the corner table beneath which his possessions lay.

For the next two hours, Homeless Guy maintained a thousand-yard-stare while sifting coffee a milliliter at a sip though his unkempt mustache.

The slush storm abated finally, just as Homeless Guy drained the last smidgen of coffee from his cup. He stood like a boulder rolling over, picked up his burdens, and shuffled toward the door.

Anxious to ditch Billy for good, I got to my feet right behind Homeless Guy's departure and followed. Billy trailed behind without any smartmouth protest. I think beneath his uncaring disdain, Burdekin's spirit chafed at his own untethered state. He wanted a new home as much as I wanted to be shut of him.

I turned up my coat collar against the continuing mingy assault from the skies. Homeless Guy was heading toward 72nd Street. At that intersection, he turned toward west toward the river.

A few blocks later, I was convinced he was heading to the greenspace along the Henry Hudson Parkway. He must camp there. Somehow that locale resonated with Billy's nature and history, and I could feel growing certainty that I had made a valid hookup. Little metaphysical evidences in Homeless Guy's gait and tics added up to further confirmation.

At the corner of the park, where the 72nd Street dog run loomed utterly empty, Homeless Guy did indeed enter the winter-bare oasis. Eager to be shed of Billy Burdekin, I hastened after Homeless Guy.

The park held no one but me and the ghost and my quarry. Homeless Guy was moving faster now, as if anxious to be back to his shelter.

Then, suddenly, he vanished among a cluster of overgrown trees.

Not wanting to lose him, I broke into a trot, and dashed among the darkened trees.

A strong forearm clotheslined me across the throat, and I went down to the wet turf.

Stupid, stupid, stupid! And sloppy! You could never let the follower know he was being followed!

I dragged air painfully into my raw throat and struggled to get up.

A foot connected with my gut. Homeless Guy was screaming abuse.

"Bastards! Robbed me once! No more!"

I tried to form some soothing words, but another kick made me swallow them. I thought it was time for a little rest, so I just stretched out in the nice cold slush. The sound of the traffic on the Henry Hudson Parkway formed a terminal lullaby.

I waited for another kick or a punch or knife thrust even, but nothing came. With immense pain, I managed to shift slightly so I could look up.

There stood Billy and the bum, but a third figure loomed in the shadows too. The new person had Homeless Guy gently restrained, using nothing more than a big hand on the wild bum's shoulder.

"That's enough now. No one wants to hurt you. Billy, why don't you go with this kind gentleman now?

"All right, sir," said Billy Burdekin, mild as milk.

Homeless Guy and Billy moved away then, down nighted paths, and the stranger turned his attention to me. He cupped me under the armpits with strong hands and lifted me up on my wobbly legs.

"My name is Pim Torens, miss. Please allow me to help."

I was going to see Pim today for the first time since I had broken up with him a month ago, and I was more than a little nervous.

Exactly how, after an antsy, half-appreciated, half-anguished separation of four weeks, do you reconnect with a guy who saved your life, slept with you on the second date (third, if you count our nearly fatal first meeting), helped you in your weird business, and didn't think you were crazy for seeing ghosts, because he could see them too?

This reunion was not going to be easy or simple.

We had arranged to meet—where else?—at a Starbucks: the branch at 1st Avenue and 75th Street. I was working at brokering a match for a ghost named Hannah Lessman, and had a gut hunch I'd find her human host in that neighborhood.

Hannah joined me as I reached the sidewalk outside my apartment.

If you took Mrs. Wilson from the *Dennis the Menace* comic strip, morphed her with Aunt Bea from the *Andy Griffith Show*, and then seasoned the result with Spidey's Aunt May, you 'd probably come fairly close to depicting Hannah Lessman. She was the kind of matronly pillow of a powder-scented, gingerbread-plump lady onto whose aproned lap you immediately wanted to rest your tired head for a soothing brow-stroking. In life she had probably smelled of vanilla extract, and in death she gave ghosts a good name. I'd be sad to lose her. But her welfare and that of her hypothetical host had to be my primary concern.

"Oh, glory!" said Hannah when she saw me. Her tone was part nervousness over our consequential errand, part disapproval of my appearance. We had engaged in, well, spirited discussions about my style of dressing before.

"What's the matter, Hannah? Don't you approve?"

I wore simple jeggings partly covered by an old Space Ghost Coast-to-Coast t-shirt, topped by a denim jacket, all quite suitable for April, I thought.

"Ladies in my day—" said Hannah, and let it go at that.

Shortly thereafter, we were walking into the Starbucks rendezvous.

When I saw Pim calmly waiting, like some visiting dignitary from a distant regal realm, all our short but intense history rushed back over me.

That December night after my assault we had exited the park, me stumbling, soaked to the skin, supported by my strong and towering rescuer. Pim said nothing after his initial offer of aid, obviously sensing I needed time to compose myself.

Out under the first streelight, I took stock of Pim Torens.

Well over six feet tall, he wore a leather jacket, black jeans and engineer boots. A mass of unruly tawny hair complemented a cheerful, concerned, craggy face and ruddy complexion. Despite the chill rain, he seemed utterly at ease.

We paused. "You are doing okay now?" he asked.

Pim Torens spoke English with a subtle accent I couldn't place. "Yes—I think so. But only because you saved me."

"It was nothing. I saw the ghost with you, and became intrigued and concerned. Billy Burdekin plainly did not consort with your nature. He could not be your personal ghost, and yet there he was, following you. So I followed too. And it was well I did."

"I owe you everything," I said, and began to cry.

Pim politely let me finishing weeping, without seeming impatient or unnerved.

"You have been doing this a long while?"

"You mean crying in front of strangers?"

He smiled. "No, I mean matchmaking with the spirits."

"About five years, more or less."

"And you have never encountered any troubles before tonight?"

I stiffened up, feeling accused of incompetence. "No! I've always been very careful and managed just fine!"

"I believe you. But there are dangers, from both mortal and spirit spheres. As I think you now realize."

"And how would you know?"

"I have been more or less in the same line of work for a very long time."

I studied the man. He looked to be about ten or fifteen years older than me, tops.

"You must have started young."

"It seems ages ago."

We resumed walking.

"Let us go inside someplace warm, and I will buy you a hot drink."

"Anyplace but Starbucks!" I said, and we both started to laugh.

The night of my rescue extended into the early morning

hours, hours spilling over with talk while my clothes dried on me in a warm diner full of good smells and a large platter of midnight breakfast food for me. Pim claimed he wasn't hungry. I told Pim everything about myself and he told me—well, enough to satisfy me for the moment.

Pim Torens was Dutch by birth, had enough money to supply his modest needs without maintaining a dayjob, lived somewhere south of City Hall, and occupied his time as I did, bringing unaffiliated ghosts and despairing humans together for their mutual benefit.

"I have found ours to be a demanding profession," he said toward dawn, as he shepherded me back to my apartment. "Perhaps you could use some help."

I felt tired and giddy and unaccountably happy for someone who had been nearly throttled and kicked to death. I didn't notice then that Pim had phrased his offer as a one-way street. "You suggesting a team-up? Go on patrol together, like Batman and Catwoman?"

"These names are not familiar to me. But, yes, I think maybe we should try working together."

"All right! You Scooby, me Velma."

Pim grinned. "Again, I confess I am at a loss. But it makes me happy if you accept my offer. I will see you again soon."

When next we met, the occasion was non-professional, just hanging out at my suggestion, to become better acquainted. We visited the Cloisters, a suitably atmospheric place, I thought, for two spookhunters. Then we did a ghost brokering together, pairing up a wispy unassuming spirit named Henry Breeding, who had shown prize bulldogs in life, with a young woman we started following when she left Juilliard. Pim's talents and mine clicked nicely, I thought, fitting together like lock and key—or maybe engine and supercharger. My intuitions and senses felt really amped up in Pim's presence.

Then came our second date, the lurid details of which I prefer to keep to myself, except to say, *Wow!*

Lying in bed afterwards, Pim said something very touching and perceptive that had me quietly weeping again.

"Ilona, I think maybe your job has made you too removed from humans. This is not good. You have not had a relationship in a long time, am I right?"

He was right, of course, and I could only be grateful that he had undone my long solo streak.

What brought Pim and me to our unfortunate interregnum, however, was a certain insufferable sense of superiority on his part, a kind of bossiness bred from his vaster experience.

He began to contradict my choices, and insist on his. Always gently, I admit, but with lots of covert forcefulness. The ghosts I wanted to work with, the humans I picked for them—none seemed optimal, according to Pim. He always knew better, and tried to force my hand, quietly arguing that his choices were superior. And maybe they were—but they weren't mine!

After several months operating together, during which I found myself defering more and more to Pim, chafing more and more, getting more and more irate, I eventually exploded. Argument, accusations, and a vow on my part not to see him until I had had time to reconsider our relationship and how it might work.

A decisive moment arriving *now*, as Hannah and I entered

the Starbucks on that April Friday afternoon.

Pim in his invariant uniform, jeans, boots and jacket, smiling broadly. Was his face a trifle beefy? Did he privilege his own undeniable talents too much? I didn't care. All I wanted to do was squeeze him and be with him and chase ghosts together.

"Hello, Hannah," said Pim in his old-fashioned manner of addressing the elderly first, be they alive or dead.

Hannah stopped short. "Oh, glory! What are you doing here?"

"Hannah, don't be frightened. I should have mentioned that Pim would be helping us. He's a friend."

The ghost sank down into a seat and fanned her face, plump insubstantial ectoplasmic hand stirring up only the ghost of a breeze. "Oh, glory!"

I sat at the table too. "So, you're looking good."

"You also, Ilona. I have missed you."

"Hell, I bet you say that to every living girl."

Pim looked disconcerted for a moment, one of the rare instances I had ever seen him nonplussed.

"Now that you've met Hannah, any candidates on your radar?"

"Not yet. Let us relax. I am sure someone will appear."

"Want something to drink?"

"No, thank you, I've had several cups while waiting."

Returning with my Strawberries & Crème Frappuccino, I launched into a line of semi-nervous chatter, bringing Pim up to date on my life without him during the past month. He listened politely, but his mind seemed elsewhere. And then he said, simply, "Over there."

I glanced in the direction his gaze indicated and saw a middle-aged guy I pegged as a doctor on his day off. Nice, upright, comfortable.

"For Hannah?"

"Yes."

"I'm not getting the vibe."

"Trust me. Please."

Pim's big blue eyes did the trick. "Okay. But I reserve the right to pull Hannah back if I disagree."

"Of course."

When Respectable Doc got up to leave, the three of us followed circumspectly.

The client indeed seemed to have no pressing duties to attend to, leading us in a sauntering fashion up and down the neighborhood, including an extensive survey of what I could swear was every single exhibit at the Met. Doc choose to eat alone in the Museum restaurant, and I grabbed a sandwich, while Pim claimed not to be hungry.

"I focus only on the client, not myself, during the match-making."

"Well, excuse me for living!"

Evening joined us, and we found ourselves at an unlikely place: the departure platform of the Aerial Tramway to Roosevelt Island.

Respectable Doc swiped through the entrance, and Pim and I chose to follow. We would have to ride the same gondola as the client, or risk losing him. Awkwardly close quarters, but I could not see that we had been "made." And I certainly did not want to abandon the hunt after all the hours invested, before being certain that Doc was or wasn't right for Hannah.

"What an out-of-the-way place to live," I whispered to Pim while we were waiting to board.

"But quiet and peaceful, I think."

Once the gondola was in motion, riding its catenary to the empurpled heavens, I was treated to the beautiful illuminated cityscape, below and on all sides, like some bejewelled Little Nemo wonderland. This was one of those too-infrequent times when I was struck anew by just how exotic and ornate and mysterious the city could be.

Once all the passengers were discharged on the island, our client turned south, with us hanging discreetly back just far enough.

"I thought most of the residential stuff was north of here," I whispered.

Pim said nothing, hot on the chase, leaving me to hurry up and follow, with Hannah drifting along.

A road ran down the western shore of Roosevelt Island, and Respectable Doc followed it.

We came to a sprawling, lighted, busy facility that proclaimed itself the Goldwater Memorial Hospital. *Aha*, I thought, *that's where he headed! Pulling a night shift.*

But no. Our client passed it and kept going.

Illumination became non-existent. No one in the world existed except Respectable Doc and us. The pavement felt broken and gritty underfoot. I stumbled once, and Pim caught me. I could see a few of the brighter stars overhead, a Manhattan rarity. Across the neon-streaked river, the United Nations reared like a postmodern sphinx. A relative hush prevailed.

We came now to a long stretch of weed-fringed chainlink fence on the inland border of the deserted road. Massive shattered structures hulked inside.

My whisper emerged hoarse and clotted. "I know this place. I read about it once in the *Times*. The ruins of the old Smallpox Hospital…"

Pim said nothing, but just steered me on.

Respectable Doc lifted aside a loose portion of fencing with knowing ease and entered the grounds of the Renwick Ruins.

I had to follow.

It was my job.

And Pim would not let me go.

Through brick-strewn weedy wasteland, and into the amorphous gullet defined by rearing gap-toothed, empty-eyed walls.

The dark courtyard, lit only by urban light pollution, was full of shadowy, waiting people, a crowd into which Respectable Doc merged unconcernedly.

Not people, I realized, but ghosts. Scores of ghosts, of all sizes and types, shifting and milling silently like a field of grain under the wind.

Hannah joined them too. Pim and I stopped.

"Ilona, would you say hello to my people?"

I, who had easily conversed one-on-one with spirits for the past five years, found myself silent at this mute massed congregation, my mouth dry as gravedust.

"I—I— What are you, Pim?"

"I am simply the oldest ghost here, Ilona. Maybe something of a leader by virtue of my age and experience, if you will. I sailed with Henry Hudson, I died when the settlement was only part of Nieuw Nederland. Now I help my younger bretheren. My human tether and support is the sadness of the whole city."

"But you—you're solid! You're real!"

"Some ghosts are. There is much you don't know, Ilona. That's why I was trying to protect you."

"Oh my god! We had sex! Am I gonna have a ghost baby?"

"I do not believe so, Ilona."

That was some relief anyhow. "What do you intend to do with me?"

"Nothing, Ilona. Nothing but what you wish. I just had to show you the truth of my life—my afterlife—if we were to continue on together."

I considered my startling new reality for a moment, before asking, "Are you hooked up with some human?"

"No, Ilona, it is as I said. The whole city is my ally."

With both hands I gripped Pim's bicep through his leather jacket. "Well, you're hooked up now."

And then, no longer ghostless, I followed him home.

In honor of Dylan Thomas's "The Followers"

The Alighted House

Elgar Allan Poe, Completed by K.J. Cypret

JAN 1 — 1796. This day — my first on the light-house — I make this entry in my Diary, as agreed on with De Grät. As regularly as I can keep the journal, I will — but there is no telling what may happen to a man all alone as I am — I may get sick, or worse .... So farewell ! The cutter had a narrow escape — but why dwell on that, since I am here, all safe? My spirits are beginning to revive already, at the mere thought of being — for once in my life at least — thoroughly alone; for, of course, Neptune, large as he is, is not to be taken into consideration as "society". Would to Heaven I had ever found in "society" one half as much faith as in this poor dog — in such case I and "society" might never have parted — even for the year . . . What most surprises me is the difficulty De Grät had in getting me the appointment — and I a noble of the realm! It could not be that the Consistory had any doubt of my ability to manage the light. One man had attended it before now — until his death — and got on quite as well as the three that are usually put in. The duty is a mere nothing; and the printed instructions are as plain as possible. It never would have done to let Orndoff accompany me. I never should have made any way with my book as long as he was within reach of me, with his intolerable gossip — not to mention that everlasting meerschaum pipe. Besides, I wish to be alone .... It is strange that I never observed, until this moment, how dreary a sound that word has — "alone"! I could half fancy there was some peculiarity in the echo of these cylindrical walls — but oh, no! — this is all nonsense. I do believe I am going to get nervous about my isolation. That will never do. I have not forgotten De Grät's prophecy. Now for a scramble to the lantern and a good look around to "see what I can see" .... To see what I can see indeed ! — not very much. The swell is subsiding a little, I think — but the cutter will have a rough passage home, nevertheless. She will hardly get within sight of the Norland before noon tomorrow — and yet it can hardly be more than 190 or 200 miles.

JAN.2

I have passed this day in a species of ecstasy that I find impossible to describe. My passion for solitude could scarcely have been more thoroughly gratified. I do not say satisfied; for I believe I should never be satiated with such delight as I have experienced to-day …. The wind lulled about day-break, and by the afternoon the sea had gone down materially …. Nothing to be seen, with the telescope even, but ocean and sky, with an occasional gull.

JAN. 3

A dead calm all day. Towards evening, the sea looked very much like glass. A few sea-weeds came in sight; but besides them absolutely nothing all day — not even the slightest speck of cloud …. Occupied myself in exploring the light-house …. It is a very lofty one — as I find to my cost when I have to ascend its interminable stairs — not quite 160 feet, I should say, from the low-water mark to the top of the lantern. From the bottom inside the shaft, however, the distance to the summit is 180 feet at least — thus the floor is 20 feet below the surface of the sea, even at low-tide …. It seems to me that the hollow interior at the bottom should have been filled in with solid masonry. Undoubtedly the whole would have been thus rendered more safe — but what am I thinking about? A structure such as this is safe enough under any circumstances. I should feel myself secure in it during the fiercest hurricane that ever raged — and yet I have heard seamen say occasionally, with a wind at South-West, the sea has been known to run higher here than anywhere with the single exception of the Western opening of the Straits of Magellan. No mere sea, though, could accomplish anything with this ponderous, iron-riveted wall — which, at 50 feet from high-water mark, is four feet thick, if one inch .... The basis on which the structure rests seems to me to be chalk ....

JAN. 4

High tide today. At dawn the ocean rolls onto the shore in teeming swells ... short intervals between each crest. A myriad of saucer size, gelatinous medusas bestrew the sand and rocks.... To the eastern horizon, a darkened sky speaks of a passing storm. I accomplish my light-house duties, mostly trimming of the wicks and re-oiling of the lantern, by midday and attempt to work on my manuscript—mindful that the only writing I have done in a fortnight is this diary...The keeper's room, really a cell, is mid-level of the shaft, and adjacent to the storeroom and pantry, is furnish with a small taboret and another chair, desk that also serves as a dining table, straw filled bed and locker, and a pantry to the side. The room is organized with great economy. In my trunk are blankets and a copy of *King James Bible* and *Belkin's Animated Nature of the Oceans.* The desk faces a narrow window, 90 feet above sea level, the sole window in the shaft. At this vantage, I see how the ocean has risen to an unusual degree. I walked to the water's edge in twenty paces, perhaps 50 feet from the door— I take no alarm in this, nor the swells awash with jelly-fishes. Silence is pervasive, and my sense of solitude is complete... perhaps due to the vicinity of the coming storm, or high tide, the gulls have abandoned the isle. Only Neptune skulks about — though he seem not pleased with the incoming tide. I return to dabbling at my book. At sun-fall the dark clouds broke away to windward for a moment, and I had the advantage of a full moon for a few minutes. That night a gale began to wail outside the light-house walls. It is impossible to describe the howlings and bellowings — as if demons were bursting forth from the bowels of the earth.

JAN. 5

This morning I awoke to the barking of Nepture and to find the sea had breached the light-house walls. The whole of the light-house cellar had been inundated over-night.... I now recognized the architectural wisdom of the light-house build-ers. The deep hollow has become a reservoir. The shaft wall was built to admit sea-water....In that way, I believe the pres-sures of the prodigious oceans are lessened. Water drains in the walls must be large enough to admit the medusas — the cellar pool is filled with them. There was no alarm to be tak-en.... quite distinctly I saw that the sea level was subsiding. A foot of sea-weed and sea-muck lined the interior walls above the water table—this is not the monotony I had expected to find here. De Grät will not be amused when he reads this. I realized that the cellar must be cleaned out before the rot and fish odor pervaded the light-house. By noon the water in the "hold" had receded to a few feet and I waded down the stairs with shovel and carpet bag in hand.... Noah had to be selec-tive in his voyage, but what of the creatures that swam in the seas? Who knows what manner of beasts survived the origi-nal flood. I can see no reason for medusas.... But, then rats made the trip aboard the Ark — surely without an invitation.... After much laboring I succeeded, at length, in removing a large portion of the jelly-fishes from the cellar. There is no identification of the *hydrozoa* in Belkins zoology.... But, I find them to be of the benign kind, unlike the Portuguese man-of-war, and suffer no blistering of hands or skin. That night, in the shadow of the moon, I noticed a luminescent glow to the wall of the cellar...I descended the stairs without my oil lamp and touched the stone wall.... The feel is that of raw whale blubber. I fixedly gazed around me, my thoughts spiraling in me as I turned my back to leave...

JAN. 6

The cellar is considerably drier today.... the shore at the level of my first day on the isle. I passed the day in a series of tasks, mostly in cleaning the light-house — the flood had left much to do.... It is at night-fall that I look anew down the stairs and first notice the foot-prints—the marks of bare feet — painted in the luminescent, climbing the stairs and fading away after a dozen steps...De Grät would say he was right, if he could have seen my ever-pacing thoughts at that moment — I remember the whole time I had been in the cellar yesterday, I had worn sea boots. Yet, they can be naught but my own feet — lurid imagination does not readily flow in me.... The only time I am without my boots is in bed.... Are the foot-marks of one asleep? The luminescent "white-wash" is also creeping out of the depths of the light-house. I can still see the level where the flood of yesterday had abated—appearing as a darkening of the mortar — and the encompassing glow has surely extended some steps higher. I can not account for the phenomenon.

JAN. 7

A week has passed since my first day on this rocky isle. The light-house up-keep has become routine...I am sleeping somewhat fitfully. This morning I brought the telescope up to the lantern deck.... In the full morning light, and from such a high perch, I believed I sighted the coast of Norway, but I knew it was only the sun rays distorting the watery horizon. It is a day when the sun is completely visible, the whole world booming before its intensity. Presently, my isolation has not increased my yearning for "society" as De Grät thought it would. I still have Neptune, always at my side. This night, confounding my soul, I admit the peculiarity of the foot-steps have remained. A second set now appears over-laying the previous fading markings.... The second set of steps following the first. The luminescence has also risen a stair-step higher, with the foot-falls. My nightly steps, for whom else's would they be, bestir uneasy thoughts in me at my nocturnal wanderings.

JAN. 8

The ocean has tossed a body ashore. Some poor soul from a ship now lying at the bottom of the sea. There can be no burial on this rocky island and I use a long pole to attempt to push it back under the waves, but have no success in this endeavor. I leave it for the tide. I believe it to be a seaman from the cutter that brought me to this place. The body had been in the water some days, and would have been impossible to identify if not for a fore-arm tattoo I recognized from a sailor aboard the cutter. I had admired a seal-skin wallet he owned, which allows me to recall his body adornment — The body bespoke the sad fate of my transport ship.

JAN. 9

I make this entry mid-day as sounding-board to my thoughts. I have passed the morning in better spirits, if not corporeality — after last night forced humor. The bottle of brandy I had brought in case of illness, now mostly gone. I doubt I could have risen from my bed at any point in time last night, under any condition. As a matter of record — every night heretofore has yielded a new series of steps to the point where at the lower level I can no longer discern new tracks from old. The storm-tossed body that washed ashore on the 8th has floated back to sea.

JAN. 10

I walked along the sandy beach at low tide with Neptune beside me—glancing downward I noticed, for the first time, the parallel paw tracks of my quadruped companion. I was startled in my realization at that moment that no such tracks have accompanied my phantom steps ascending the light-house.… I find my imagination most readily assented to all manner of the supernatural.

JAN. 11

After my daily work I have made many observations today of the structure of the light-house. Although well built, it is not, I think, a sound structure. I scrutinized the strange cellar, still damp from the last storm, and closely examined the stone-work. It is impossible to see the mortar used in the piling of stone upon stone. The skill in the construction almost seems to belong to an age before our modern times and parallels, I think, that of the pyramids. The peculiar character about the structure strikes me as rendered for a purpose beyond the building's immediate function. I cannot find any drains or channels and I am at a loss to explain the presence of the medusas.

JAN. 12

Horror today. Neptune brought me a human hand in his mouth. He ran off when I attempted to take it away from him. I rushed outside the light-house to find him. The general surface of the ocean was somewhat more level than the stormy days hereunto, and it took me a moment to see it. A longboat, as if freshly formed out of air, beached and a dead man within it. The boat and man inside had received considerable injury, his bandaged wrist told me all I needed to know about Neptune's toy. The boat was completely water-logged with only one oar in evidence, and it took me a moment before I perceived a second passenger lying in the bow… a woman. At first her sodden and torn dress gave the appearance of a hastily rolled-up sail. It was a while before I could reason myself into sufficient courage to approach the boat. The woman still breathed, but was unconscious. It was a miracle she escaped destruction, though she appeared more dead than alive. With much effort I carried her into the light-house and gave her water when she awoke briefly. When I returned to the boat it was gone, carried away with the tide. The dead sailor had done his duty then returned to his ship, God knows how many fathoms below. Neptune has disappeared behind the light-house.

JAN. 14

I do not know where I can find a better place than here to make mention of one or two things. First: Though I had some vague idea of the perils of this occupation, or those perils straightforwardly presented to me by De Grät, yet I thought from the beginning that the frequency with which they occur would be ever so slight. Yes, of actual disasters and deaths on the high-seas not one in fifty ever finds a public record. I expect that these odds decrease in proximity to land. But those odds, I think, are no worse than that of being tossed by a horse and breaking one's neck. Yes, this is just a rock in the vast ocean and not a ship – still this minuscule rock has the hazards of any ship riding on the waves…. Many books of old-fashioned manly adventures are full of the courage of sailors on ships. I see them not as heroes – just toilers on the earth, the same as a farmer or hunter. De Grät is wrong, I did not come here to prove my bravery. I could never quite explain to him my experience of the diabolism of nature. Second: This rock is my own ship and I am its captain, and a captain must not take his responsibilities lightly. Just as nature can send a storm to batter and sink a ship it can as easily batter this island under the waves. But that is not what I fear.

JAN. 15

I now have a guest in the light-house. At first I thought the wan creature delivered at my doorstop would soon be dead. The present situation is not an arrangement that agrees with me. I have given my guest the bed where I slept and now sleep on a hard cot beside the lantern. I must cover my eyes with a knotted kerchief to block the flame light and awake in the morning covered in black carbon and smelling of grease. The keeper's room will accommodate two persons easily but I thought it best to let the woman have the room all to herself, lest there be any awkwardness. The sea is calm after the tempest. The same can not be said of my state of mind. She has been asleep for more than twenty-four hours. A nice position for a castaway: Her body solidly planted in my bed. I announce my descent from the tower before treading on to the stairs. The woman does not respond so I step noisily. I must get to the room to prepare breakfast. She is awake and sitting in my chair at the table with Neptune quietly beside her. Her first appraisal of me seems to be one of recognition even though she had been unconscious when I brought her into the light-house. I ask her how she feels and she tells me she is reasonably well. I have a sense that the present situation is the making of a familiar novel. Her name is Livia, she is Dutch but speaks English very well. I asked her if she is comfortable and she tells me my room is as snug as a womb. I tell her that we are both marooned on this island until the next supply ship arrives. She had the table covered with my big map. The mainland does not seem too far off she tells me. Yes, I say, maps are deceptive that way, everything looks close by, but the trip by sea is dictated by commercial concerns and weather. You must be hungry, I say, and get to work in the pantry…. I prepare smoked fish and biscuits, but she does not eat…. After the meal she told me, in a halting manner, the story of the final days of the cutter. How the sea and sky became the same dark color and there was no definition between the two. Sailors possess melancholic spirits and know that if you want to sail the seas, death is always near, and there are many omens of imminent destruction. All the signs of dire foreboding were there: The air, the water, even the ship itself. The sailors heard the sound of the ship's planks wailing like the coming of Armageddon. Now, all sailors know that more ships are wrecked than return safely home, but a tremendous thunderbolt directly over our heads that snaps the mast in two and crashes onto the Captain and First Mate was the final herald for the sailors who now panicked and began to let out the longboats. Our ship heaved and the waves appeared as cliffs and the *Catterina*, without a helmsman, rode those waves like a heavy log. All the sailors abandoned the cutter. In the turmoil a good-hearted sailor, who was on the quarterdeck with the Captain when the mast came down, made room for me and my maid on the last boat. He was injured and we barely made it to the water…. his hand was crushed and was useless for rowing. (I shuddered to think where that hand was now.) The hapless cutter was caught in a vortex and went under the waves as quickly and easily as a porpoise. (Here the woman contradicts herself, as she also later reports one detail of seeing the bowsprit pointing at the sky as the ship sinks bit by bit.) They floated in the longboat for what seemed a week on rough seas with the maid disappearing one night, apparently fallen over-board. The good-hearted sailor faded and became a phantom that only saw the imminence of death. Providence and the ebb and flow of the sea brought us back here. Livia ended her story with the sighting of the light-house.

I told her it must indeed be Providence that had allowed her to survive. After telling her tale there was silence. After breakfast my castaway asked about the construction of the light-house. She told me she had never been inside such a building — she had spent all of her time below deck on the voyage out to the light-house and spied me when I first set foot on the island. I thought she was concerned about the light-house surviving a tempest and allayed her fears by assuring her of the soundness of the gray walls surrounding us. The questions she asked showed her to be a woman of some intelligence. That night Lady Livia told me that the island seemed besieged by jelly-fish. Indeed their umbrella-like gelatinous forms were everywhere one turned when walking along the shore-line.

JAN. 16

Able now to stand on her feet and walk around, I could see that in stature Lady Livia was tall, somewhat slender…. At dusk she ventured out of the light-house with Neptune. As I toiled at my duties I descended to the ground floor and saw that the door to the cellar was open and across its inner side a hand had scrawled in the luminescent paint: I was here *I Am Here*. The lettering is not my script, and I do not recognize the calligraphy. Until this moment I had not thought of the light-house keeper who preceded me. *Is the handwriting of the previous keeper?* In these jottings I will not pretend to have full knowledge of the things that happened before my time here. My little diary happens to contain a few jottings referring to the conversation I had with De Grät in December, a week before Christmas, which may cast a light on the subject of the previous light-house keeper. De Grät told me the story of the week that the light in the tower was seen to burn day and night, and when a ship was sent to investigate it was discovered that the keeper had died in a fall down the staircase. No one could explain how the lamp burned for so long an interval without a keeper to replenish the oil. I have always taken pride in my tepid atheism, so the present-day notion of nebulous spirits, weaned from the sacramental worship in our churches, is to my thinking, obsolete in this modern age.... I have thought of this place as corporeal confinement where the mind is at liberty and now find it a prison for a spectre.... But only a religious mind could contemplate that. [It is tempting to go back and rewrite my Diary, but this is not my manuscript, and I feel compelled to under-score my calmness at this stage.] I once asked De Grät what all lunatics he knew had in common. He described some of the many delusions he has seen in a few of his patients and said the only thing they all had in common was their certitude. "I believe many of them want to peel off a dreary and unhappy past and replace it with an exultant invention. Yet there were some whose invention was of a higher visionary order and not easily put out-of-mind."

I can doubt many things — but not the evidence of my own eyes. My first impulse, of course, was to ask Lady Livia if she had written the message on the door. I waited for the proper moment, after our dinner. Asking the question prompted me

to give her an account of the phenomenon of the past fortnight. She heard me to the end — and at first stared at me
with an attitude of the profoundest attention — then lapsed
into a grave demeanor, as if my sanity was under suspicion. I
took her to the bottom of the edifice to show her the markings,
but she maintained that she could see nothing — and I admit
that the markings had greatly faded — though I pointed out
the course of the footsteps and the very spot where the writing was on the door-frame. I was immeasurably alarmed, for
now I considered the vision either an omen of foreboding, or,
worse, as the fore-runner of an attack of mania. I threw myself passionately back from the cellar, and for some moments
buried my face in my hands. When I uncovered my eyes Lady
Livia questioned me rigorously. She had the mind of a sci-
entist and had also noted that the cellar excavation lay at an
excessive depth below the surface of the earth. She had also
noticed that no outlet was observed in any portion of its vast
cavity, and no source of light was discernible; yet a sort of light
flooded throughout the cellar-vault of the light-house, and
bathed the whole in a ghastly and inapt splendor. Lady Livia
endeavored to have me believe that much, if not all of what I
felt, was due to the bewildering influence of the gloomy tower,
the dark days without company, the dead seaman, and the
savage aspect of the island. Yet, I am not hypochondriacal in
mind nor do I have a fail body. She reminded me of my noble
birth and endeavored to arouse me from the pitiable condition into which I had fallen. I still retained sufficient presence
of mind to allay her fears for my sanity.

JAN. 17

This day, the commencement of the third day of her stay on the island, the Lady Livia fell into a sudden illness. I watched her with feelings of anxiety. The fever that consumed her gave way to moments of fancy when she spoke of phantasmagoric influences in the light-house. She believes she heard steps on the stairs belonging to bare feet while I was in the room sitting beside her…. I heard nothing. A fever dream, but I think that we all possess perceptions attuned to different standards. It must be so…. It might have been midnight, as she slept fitfully, when I took a step to the door of the keeper's room and looked down the staircase. It was not a sound that I heard but a presence I felt. In an agony of superstitious terror I strained my vision to detect any motion from below. Neptune sat still beside the bed, where the Lady Livia lay in what seemed a cataleptic state. I could see nothing from my vantage point and would have to descend to see better — this I could not venture to do. Some time elapsed when I became aware of some vague manifestation from the region of the cellar. Again I went to the door and directed my sight below. This time I waited a long interval and my eyes grew accustomed to the dim light. (What marvel that I do not shudder while I write). After this there was a dead stillness, the flame of a candle burned upon the desk without the least perceptible motion, and I saw and felt nothing more. Neptune was awake, but seem unperturbed and I believe his vigilance allowed me to fall asleep before daybreak, not without a full presentiment of evil.

JAN. 18

It may seem strange that in spite of the continual anxiety I continued to function. It is difficult, indeed, to define my real emotions here on this fair page. Was it that in the company of women even pusillanimous men are capable of performing stirring acts of bravery? With my castaway I felt an uneasy curiosity along with a feeling of vexation that grew stronger with each passing day. Today I sped through my light-house labors quickly. I took some time to attend to the Lady Livia, though there was little I could do for her, and she appeared no better in the afternoon. The pallor of her countenance had assumed, if possible, a more ghastly hue. If I had the proper medical tools, and knowledge, I would have bled her. It would be an easy matter to discuss her symptoms, but I forbore out of decency toward the Lady, my own modesty, and lack of medical wisdom. Her fever still raged, and she had fallen into a state of stupor. I could not offer any means of relief. I had not thought to bring medical books with me, though, I believe, they would have been of little use without academic guidance. Perhaps it is time that I write of my keenness to seek solitude to better explain my occupancy in this light-house on this entirely secluded, and inaccessible, rock in the middle of the sea. I have always been fearful of my fellow man.... and to be honest, women. De Grät thought that through a physical isolation, a sort of holiday from other people, I would grow to crave the company of humanity and thereby be cured of my fears. But I have found no isolation here.... and indeed have only been thrown into closer quarters with the corporeal component of humanity.... as well as a phantom as an uninvited guest.

Neptune now barks and flees the room whenever I enter.

JAN. 19

This morning a crisis ... the Lady has taken a turn for the worse and appears to be in a death-like statew — wounds are visible on her wrists and neck as in a blood letting. In my mind I am not the agent of these wounds. Could I have done this in some sleep-walking condition? Perhaps those are my steps in the stairwell — that sanity should run aground on such a place, and wrecked all reason out of me .... I only see an ineffable end, and lurid woe flows in me. I remember horrible old De Grät's jocular prophesy that I could go to the light-house and leave it mad.... My natural philosophy of Pyrrhonism has been shaken these past few weeks.

JAN. 20

The Lady has been attacked in the night. I find her on the floor beside the bed.

JAN. 21

Neptune is dead .... He reared to do violence to me when I entered the Lady's room this morning and I grasped a pantry knife to defend myself.... Poor Neptune.... It is my plan to take the small boat and row out to the sea to remove myself from the company of the Lady. I will serve as the ferryman Charon and take Neptune with me. The supply ship is due on the morrow and, with God's grace, they will find her alive even if my disappearance will be a mystery. I know that these pages will be read as the ravings of a madman. I only pray that the invisible phantom is not a doppelganger, or the malevolent spirit of the previous keeper, and my absence only allows the thing to do its evil without restraint…. I see no other recourse. If I jeopardize my immortal soul it will be for my conscious sins, and not those committed as a sleeping fiend. As I write these final words distinctly visible outside the window is the ocean full with many thousands of the medusa, that appear as wraiths in the moon-less night …. Many are washed up in the beach like a velvet carpet. I will take my leave at midnight. They will light my way.

Item from the *Newport Mercury Weekly Journal*, February 14, 1796: A provision ship stopping at the Boddington Rock Light-house off the coast of Norland found its newly placed keeper missing and the small island completely without any habitant. It is believed that the keeper was under some mental duress and abandoned his station in a small boat, taking a pet dog with him. The keeper had replaced the previous keeper who had died in the light-house in an accident. In a parallel turn of fate the cutter *Catterina*, which transported the keeper to the light-house, foundered in a storm, days after leaving the island, with all aboard lost at sea.

In honor of Elgar Allan Poe

Footfall

_____

Gay Partington Terry

"A cage went in search of a bird." — Franz Kafka, *Aphorisms*, 1918

I came into this world feet first. Loved as a child, I was spoiled and fussed over. We were not well off, but I was rich in attention. I had mother, father, aunts, cousins, grandmothers who fawned over me, uncles who admired me. I lived in a circle of warmth. I had privileges and was disciplined gently or, more often, not at all. The ground at my feet was solid and unmoving, the sky protective. The world offered itself up. I had only to stand firm and open my arms to receive it, or run freely through it.

But life as an adult, was not so benevolent. It nibbled at my tender toes, and like a hookworm, crawled beneath my skin. It penetrated my digestive tract, poisoned my organs and fed on my mind. I attempted to hold tight and project an air of unconcern, to abide with dignity. But it pinched my metatarsals and inflamed my flexors.

When the foundational extremity is assaulted, the footing compromised, the entire structure declines. It wobbles uncontrollably. I became demanding, elitist. People pushed away from me and I was indifferent. Common codes didn't apply to me. Not me. Surely.

I acknowledge hatred. I lied. I manipulated. I took. I felt justified. The death of my immediate family left me free to do what I had never dreamed of doing in their presence.

I lost all, knowingly. I accepted the loss of all that was honorable— even forfeited the trust of thieves.

One morning I looked about my once tasteful rooms and saw broken objects and bloody clothes cluttering the floor. I was dirty and disheveled; my body bruised, scraped, cut. My feet, previously well cared for, were blemished and flayed. For the first time in many weeks, I must have slept because I had a dream. If only I could remember what it was about the dream that changed me. If I could brush the boundaries within that dream one more time…If only…

I began a ritual cleansing.

I purged my luxurious apartment of everything unnecessary to the extent of walling off all but three of the smaller rooms: kitchen, bath and study. I found money that I'd hidden, telephoned the corner store for food and supplies. I sealed the windows, locked the doors, battened myself in against enemies.

At the end of each day, I sat in the weathered chair by my window with the lights out.

From my rooms I could see directly across to the window he might jump out of. It was cracked but unsoiled and had a small ledge he might crawl out on, to contemplate his options had he any to contemplate.

He never left his rooms. He received no visitors. He sat in his chair or busied himself with small tasks. He had only one light but for the glow of his TV. He washed his clothes out in the sink and hung them on the shower rod, barely visible from my vista.

I had an ample view into his sad life and though I pitied him, I had no inclination to help or interfere with his bleak destiny (were such a thing possible).

It amused me to watch his struggle. He became my own personal ant farm, scratching endlessly but unable to escape his lot. (This, of course, is an unfair comparison — he wasn't nearly as industrious as an ant.) Though his TV was always on providing company, he often sat at the window staring at his ledge and beyond with a stunned look. I wondered if he was aware that I was watching.

Studying him lessened my anxiety. I began to contemplate the notion that I might have been forgotten. Where were my enemies, the people I'd lied to, cheated, robbed, scammed, abused, damaged, deserted? Why didn't they seek revenge, as I would have? Perhaps they'd fallen as far as I, and no longer had the means… or the strength.

After a while, I became curious about that part of his life I couldn't see from my window. I kept my TV on in an attempt to ascertain what he might be watching. I could see only flashing light and scanning patterns due to the angle of his receiver.

I attempted to reconcile these to more significant images on my own screen.

With powerful binoculars I observed other aspects of his piteous life: the faded shirts he favored, the worn jeans; his choice of cuisine—cereals, canned tuna, raisons, butter biscuits, coffee—not unlike my own preferred provisions. I contemplated the obsessive ordering and preening of his meager dominion.

I was able to ascertain many details, but was frustrated by one fundamental aspect that remained concealed. I couldn't see what he wore on his feet.

The feet were always positioned at an angle below or just out of my vision. The defining element of personality was missing, rendering me unable to analyze the crucial detail of his mean life. Did he shuffle about in worn slippers like me? Did he wear street shoes in order to sound more substantial and alert his downstairs neighbor as to his existence? Were his feet deformed in such a way that required corrective shoes? Were they in a condition that compelled him to pad about bare, despite a cold floor? Did he move through life in shoes that were expensive? Custom made? Perhaps he purchased shoddy footwear from the sale bin at ValueMart. Did they slip on the feet easily? Tie? Or, horrors, Velcro?

I was dismayed by the vast footwear possibilities, the gravity of choice and his success at concealing this most significant clue to his character.

It forced me to become more vigilant. I expanded my surveillance and included intermittent sightings at odd hours.

It was maddening! From my vantage, there was no footwear visible anywhere in his apartment. At any time.

I studied my own meager collection. What remained after massive purging efforts, I kept hidden beneath floorboards so as not to be left without means of escape in case of emergency. Saditha Nova walking shoe, lightweight and flexible, the best money could buy; Timberland UberPros, thick leather, steel-cap toe, waterproof, excellent traction; custom-made moccasins, comfortable, historically veracious; and the yak-fur slippers that I don every morning, irreplaceable as they'd been made by a cobbler in Shanghai, now deceased. I considered the implication of the substantial contour left on the inner-sole, the curve of an arch, the imprint of metatarsal, bunion, spur; a worn outer sole or heel indicating a personality moving forward or stubbornly attached; side wear betraying left leaning or right. The care one takes of the shoe—polishing, repairing, storage… Nature and temperament revealed by footwear.

Without thinking, I tore up the floorboards, stepped out of my slippers and into the moccasins, rendering myself snug, silent and lightweight. I donned my all-weather Burberry over jeans and tee and, for the first time in many months, unlocked the front door.

I hesitated only a moment before sallying down the stairwell and out into the night air without acknowledging the shocked nod of the concierge on duty. I strode boldly across the street unrecognized by agents, (surely there were well concealed agents sent by my adversaries), through the derelict lobby of that opposing building, past a distracted doorkeeper, and up the dim and shaky stairwell to the fourteenth floor. A single window at the end of the peeling corridor offered orientation, enabling me to establish the probable location of the apartment I sought.

I turned the knob and the door opened. The inside was dark but for the light of the TV. I'm sure I heard a choked gasp, a chair scrape, footsteps. I felt the rush of air as he passed me. The door slammed before I could see… Had I perceived the sound of unshod feet? Crepe soles? Moccasins similar to my own? Perhaps speed and partial contact with the floor had disguised the sound of a more substantial shoe. I rushed to follow.

But the door stuck and slowed me down.

There was no one in the hallway, no sound in the stairwell when I reached it. I ran back into the apartment and with much effort, opened the window, leaned out over the ledge and scanned the street for a full twenty minutes.

Nothing.

Leaving the door ajar, I searched the building to no avail except to restore appreciation for the custom moccasins I'd previously underemployed. Their comfort and stealth attributes were utterly satisfying.

I returned to the stranger's apartment.

The TV, having been disturbed in the confusion, was dislodged and emitted only rolling scintillation and static, no way to tell what he'd been watching. I proceeded to switch on the only light. I drew down thick blinds and heavy curtains and though I searched for many hours, I was unable to locate one item of footwear. Not one! He'd left only a few items of clothing behind. These I washed out in the sink and hung in the bathroom. I did this in the event that I might need them. For, after hours of searching, I peeked out the window in order to access his perspective, and across the street in the apartment opposite — one I assumed to be mine — I saw movement. Enemy? Stalker? Had the displaced object of my obsession invaded my rooms as I had intruded upon his? Could it be..? The apartments might be interchangeable, can the inhabitants be likewise? Would he become the target of my enemies? Were those enemies afoot?

I'm not overly concerned as yet since the stranger has a large inventory of food and cleaning supplies which I discovered by careful reconnaissance. I've locked myself in. I've repaired the TV and am searching for suitable emissions. On close examination, I've discovered an area of flooring, recently disturbed, loose and unprofessional in formation. I've taken time to contemplate the purpose of such a fabrication. A contained area of damage or wear that was repaired haphazardly? The contour of a resistant stain?

I believe it more likely a badly camouflaged hiding place. I savor the disclosure when it's opened. What valuables will I find? Perhaps there are victims concealed within? Espionage paraphernalia? Above all, I pray it contains the telltale footwear his refuge lacks.

In honor of Franz Kafka

Acknowledgements

Our thanks goes out to all the supporters of this project: Ned Brooks, Pat and Les Cohen, J. Crimi, Beret Elway, Karen Kenny, Rob Kline, Lucas K. Law, John F. Maselli, Todd Mason, Alexandra Ortiz, Robert Sedler, Ruth Van Alst, George Wechsler, and all the people who chose to be anonymous.

Authors

DAMIEN BRODERICK is a writer whose works include the novel *The Judas Mandala* and critical studies *Ferocious Minds* and *X, Y, Z, T: Dimensions of Science Fiction*. He is a five-time recipient of the Australian SF Ditmar Award and a runner-up for the John W. Campbell Memorial Award for Best Science Fiction Novel. His *Science Fiction: The 101 Best Novels 1985-2010*, edited with Paul Di Filippo is available from Nonstop Press. He lives in San Antonio, Texas.

K.J. CYPRET is the editor of the *Nonstop Book of Fantastika Tattoo Designs*.

SCOTT EDELMAN has published more than 75 short stories in magazines such as *Postscripts, The Twilight Zone Magazine, Absolute Magnitude, Science Fiction Review* and *Fantasy Book*, and in anthologies such as *The Solaris Book of New Science Fiction. What Will Come After*, a collection of his zombie fiction, and *What We Still Talk About*, a collection of his science fiction stories, were both published this year. He has been a Stoker Award finalist five times, in the categories of both Short Story and Long Fiction. *What Will Come After* is currently a Shirley Jackson Award nominee in the category of single-author collection.

IVAN FANTI is an online freelance writer who is a fan of pseudonyms. His name here may be one too, though the name on the check we wrote him has the letters LLC at the end, which may be a good reason for the use of a pen-name. He lives in Long Island City near the Queensborough Bridge. He tells us, "I will never call it the Ed Koch Bridge."

PAUL DI FILIPPO is a two-time Nebula Award finalist and a Philip K. Dick finalist. He is the author of *The Steampunk Trilogy, Top Ten: Beyond the Farthest Precinct*, and *Creature from the Black Lagoon*. His most recent book is *The Great Jones Coop Ten Gigasoul Party*. He lives in Providence, Rhode Island.

GARY LOVISI is the publisher behind Gryphon Books and the editor of the long-running *Paperback Parade*. He edited *Bad Girls Need Love, Too*. His most recent book is *The Winged Men*. He lives in Brooklyn.

ALIGRIA LUNA LUZ was born in Ponces, Puerto Rico, and moved to Brooklyn when she was fifteen. Aligria won't say what year that was. She is working on a novel about Madame Blavatsky and the great Roberto Clemente.

BARRY MALZBERG is the author of over fifty books that encompass mystery, science fiction, movie novelizations, and literary pornography, the latter for the infamous Olympia Press. He most recent book is *The Very Best of Barry N. Malzberg* from Nonstop Press. He was born in Brooklyn and now lives across the Hudson River in Teaneck, New Jersey.

LUIS ORTIZ is an editor, artist and author based in New York City. He was nominated for the Hugo and Locus award for *Emshwiller: Infinity X Two*, and is the author most recently of *Outermost: The Art + Life of Jack Gaughan*. Forthcoming from him will be *The Steampunk Coloring Book*.

PAIGE QUAYLE: "My family's been in this country a long time, hundreds of years — well, at least one hundred. They came from places like Northern Ireland and England as indentured servants and worked their way up to become tenant farmers. They were poor, but mostly upstanding folk. Farmers are middle-class where I came from. In the years they were here they married everybody: Dutch, Welsh, Slavic, even a Seneca Indian. They drew the line at Italians which is sad because it certainly would have improved the bloodline and Sunday dinners." The peripatetic Paige lives in the Bronx these days — in a Latino neighborhood.

STEVE RASNIC TEM is the author of close to 400 published short stories and is a past winner of the Bram Stoker, International Horror Guild, British Fantasy, and World Fantasy Awards.

GAY PARTINGTON TERRY has published stories in the *Fortean Bureau, Lady Churchill's Rosebud Wristlet, The Twilight Zone Magazine, Full Spectrum*, and other journals. Her story collection *Meeting the Dog Girls* is available from Nonstop Press. She lives in upper Manhattan.

DON WEBB'S unique short stories have appeared in numerous genre magazines. He lives in Austin, Texas.

OTHER BOOKS FROM NONSTOP PRESS

Lord of Darkness by Robert Silverberg
Trade paper $17.95 (ISBN: 978-1-933065-43-4; *ebook available*)

"... gripping and compulsively readable." — George R.R. Martin

SET in the 17th century and based on a true-life historical figure, this novel is a tale of exotic lands, romance, and hair-raising adventures. Andrew Battell is a buccaneer on a British ship when he is taken prisoner by Portuguese pirates. Injured and ailing, Andrew is brought to the west coast of Africa where his only solace is Dona Teresa, a young woman who nurses him back to health. Andrew's sole hope to return home is to first serve his Portuguese masters, but it is a hope that dwindles as he is pulled further and further into the interior of the continent, into the land of the Jaqqa — the region's most fierce and feared cannibal tribe — overseen by the powerful Lord of Darkness. This story demonstrates the timelessness of any great adventure and the determination to persevere at any cost.

The Very Best of Barry N. Malzberg Introduction by Joe Wrzos

Trade paper $14.95 (ISBN: 978-1-933065-41-0; *ebook available*)

FOR NEARLY half a century Barry N. Malzberg has been stretching the boundaries of science fiction and fantasy. Each of the 37 stories in this compilation offers Malzberg's trademark vision of a future that is equal parts cautionary tale and social commentary. These hand-picked selections exhibit his versatile imagination and the dark humor so characteristic of his work.

Meeting the Dog Girls, stories by Gay Partington Terry
Trade paper $14.95 (ISBN 978-1933065-20-5; *ebook available*)

"... nonpareil fantastika that will stay with you for a long time."
— *Asimov's Science Fiction Magazine*

A THIEF, languishing in prison for stealing moments, escapes and becomes a chronometric fugitive. Women wait in a long, endless line, night and day, without knowing what is at the beginning of the line. An otherworldly marble called the Ustek Cloudy passes through the hands of Ambrose Bierce, Amelia Earhart, and D. B. Cooper just before they each disappear off the face of the earth. Whether they are called fantasy, magical realism, science fiction, or brilliant parodies, the stories in this collection—the first from Gay Terry—blend the real and the fantastic in an imaginative and mischievous way. Written in the tradition of Ray Bradbury, Angela Carter, and Neil Gaiman, these contemporary fables present remarkable characters trapped in unusual situations.

The Collected Stories of Carol Emshwiller Vol. 1

$29.95 Hardcover (ISBN: 978-1-933065-22-9; *ebook available*)

"... offers not only hours of pleasure through its dozens of wonderful, magical stories, but also the rare joy of seeing a master's work develop over decades."
— *Strange Horizons*

A MASSIVE NEW COLLECTION of 88 stories. Carol Emshwiller's fiction cuts a straight path through the landscape of American literary genres: mystery, speculative fiction, magic realism, western, slipstream, fantasy and of course science fiction. Arranged chronologically, this landmark collection, the first of two volumes, allows the reader to see Emshwiller's development as a writer and easily recognize her as a major voice in the literary landscape.

Musings and Meditations: Essays and Thoughts by Robert Silverberg
Trade paper $18.95 (ISBN: 978-1-933065-20-5; *ebook available*)

"This delightful collection reflects Silverberg's wide-ranging interests, wit, and mastery of the craft." — *Publishers Weekly* (Starred Review)

A NEW COLLECTION of essays from one of contemporary science fiction's most imaginative and acclaimed wordsmiths shows that Robert Silverberg's nonfiction is as witty and original as his fiction. No cultural icon escapes his scrutiny, including fellow writers such as Robert Heinlein, Arthur C. Clarke, H. P. Lovecraft, and Isaac Asimov.

Why New Yorkers Smoke edited by Luis Ortiz

Trade paper $14.95 (ISBN: 978-1-933065-24-3; *ebook available*)

SUBTITLED; *New Yorkers Have Many Things to Fear: Real and Imagined*. This collection of original stories answers the question "What is there to fear in New York City?," with fiction from Paul di Filippo, Scott Edelman, Carol Emshwiller, Lawrence Greenberg, Gay Partington Terry, Don Webb, and Barry Malzberg, among others. The contributors represent a combination of New Yorkers, ex-New Yorkers, and wannabe New Yorkers, and their tales of fear all use New York City as an ominous backdrop. Blending the genres of fantasy, science fiction, and horror, the stories in this anthology showcase work from up-and-coming writers as well as veterans of fantastical fiction.

Steampunk Prime: A Vintage Steampunk Reader
Edited by Mike Ashley, with a foreword by Paul di Filippo, illustrated by Luis Ortiz.

Trade paper $15.95 (ISBN 978-1933065182; *ebook available*)

"These tales have the pulpy goodness steampunk fans adore...."
— *Publishers Weekly*

"Within this collection, readers will find romance, mystery, adventure, and, of course, the iconic steampunk airship." — *School Library Journal*

Science Fiction: The 101 Best Novels —1985-2010
by Damien Broderick and Paul Di Filippo.

Trade paper $14.99 (ISBN: 978-1-933065-39-7; *ebook available*)

"If you want to know the essential science-fiction books to read that were published in the last 25 years, this is your go-to guide." — *Kirkus*

INSPIRED by David Pringle's landmark volume, SCIENCE FICTION: THE 100 BEST NOVELS, which appeared in 1985, this volume will supplement the earlier selection with the authors' choice of the best SF novels issued in English during the past quarter-century. David Pringle provides a foreword.

www.nonstoppress.com